THE LADY AND THE IRON HAND

IRON HAND'S BRIDE - BOOK THREE

AYCEE MASTERSON

Published by Blushing Books
An Imprint of
ABCD Graphics and Design, Inc.
A Virginia Corporation
977 Seminole Trail #233
Charlottesville, VA 22901

Aycee Masterson
The Lady and the Iron Hand

eBook ISBN: 978-1-64563-583-3
Print ISBN: 978-1-64563-611-3
v2

Cover Art by ABCD Graphics & Design

To my boys, with all my love

A WELCOMING HOME

$\mathcal{I}$t was an unnaturally warm evening near the late end of March when Elena Isarnon heard the news: the Lord of the House, her husband Hugh, was coming home.

"Finally!" Elena was elated to hear the news. After dismissing the messenger, she sat up and clapped her hands. "Sybil! Sybil!" The Lady called for her maidservant, then climbed out of bed and made it to her feet with an immense effort, clenched teeth, and the assistance of a conveniently placed chair she'd propped nearby for just that reason. "Is everything ready?" She couldn't just leave the confines of her bedchamber in naught but her nightgown, so Elena threw a thin shawl about her shoulders for decency's sake.

"Coming, Milady, coming!" Sybil hurried in with a flurry of skirts and excitement; the woman was a bubbling torrent of energy and anticipation, like a swollen bottle whose cork was ready to pop at any second. "But you shouldn't be up on your feet now! If milord sees you out of bed–"

"Nonsense." Elena waved a hand in dismissal as she held out a hand for Sybil to take. "He'll worry me into an early grave at this rate. If I spend one more minute in that bed, I'm liable to be swallowed up by it and never be heard from again. Now, help me."

Sybil was a pretty, busty brunette, the same age but taller than plain, mouse-haired Elena. She was also the closest thing to a friend her mistress had—they'd known each other for more than a decade, ever since Elena became the unwilling wife of Lord Isarnon and Sybil was summoned to work as a maidservant. Quickly and obediently, the other woman hurried to her Lady's side and offered an arm and shoulder to grab hold of, helping Elena to stand a little taller, easing the immense strain on her lower back.

"Oh, Heavens," Elena said, sighing. "That is... a little better." She passed a hand across her distended stomach. It'd taken a good many years for her fallow belly to finally bear fruit, and now its apparent overabundance was driving her crazy—she'd never felt so big as she did then. "How on *earth* do other women do this sort of thing over and over again?" She expelled a wordless sigh of frustration as she started waddling for the bedroom door and the slow, agonizing journey to the main hall at the front of the house. "And to think that Isolda and Gerald are on their fifth youngling by now. I swear, the woman is superhuman."

"Sixth, actually, Milady," Sybil offered helpfully. Isolda was head cook in the kitchens, her man, Gerald, in charge of the Lord's stables. Of course, Sybil would be the one to know how many children they had better than anyone else in the whole house—as the Lady's head maidservant, it was her job to know such things.

"Six already? God save me from such a fate," Elena said with a moan. "I haven't even managed to survive *one* yet."

"I imagine Isolda got better at it with more practice, Milady," Sybil said, pursing her mouth into a tight bow as both women started for the bedroom door. "Has the little Lordling been especially bad today?" she asked, rubbing her Lady's belly in a sympathetic manner. People seemed to think doing so would provide Elena with good luck, something she had resigned herself to long ago.

"Bad, I'll say he's been bad," Elena answered in a growl. "He refuses to sit still for more than a moment anymore. If I survive all of the cracked ribs he's kicking, I might still expire if he ever tries boxing my bladder again. And I can't remember the last time I got a full night's rest." She wanted to spit, but contented herself with another growl. "Next time, I may just get my Lord a dog and have done with it."

"Mmm," Sybil hummed in sympathy, sounding more like she hoped to satisfy her Lady than out of any real agreement.

The walk was slow and sent Elena's feet to throbbing. She looked down and sighed, not knowing what hurt more those days—her swollen feet or her aching back.

"Slowly now," Sybil said, "just one step at a time."

"At this rate, I should just sleep in the hall," Elena said. "By the time I get there, it'll be time to go right back to that infernal bed again."

"Come now, Milady. I would think you'd enjoy going to bed, seeing as that's what got you into this mess in the first place."

"Sybil!" Elena stopped and felt a hot rush in her face, and it burned twice as hot when the other woman laughed.

"Only teasing, Milady, think nothing of it." Sybil squeezed Elena's arm, then rubbed her back with a smile. Eventually, they walked into the proper front hall of the stone keep.

Hugh's Hall was vast enough that half of Corfe's citizens could easily fit inside its walls, and had done so on many previous occasions. Tomorrow would be Easter Sunday, officially marking the end of Lent, as well as the end of a traditional, four-week fasting period that barred the consumption of meat, milk, cheese and eggs, as well as the rather offensive—in Elena's opinion—prohibition on married couples partaking in sexual intercourse. Due to her pregnancy, Elena was excluded from any dietary restrictions, and she saw very little reason why the Almighty would even care about the intimate particulars of her relationship to her husband. While always considering herself a faithful daughter of the Church, Elena was sure that whatever fool had decided that starving one's self brought them closer to God obviously never had to carry a baby around while doing so.

Tomorrow would also mark a celebratory feast day for the whole town, and the great kitchens of Lord Isarnon's house were cooking up a meal of massive proportions. Hugh was known throughout all of Dorsetshire and the surrounding counties for his generosity, and while the town's citizens were both welcomed and encouraged to bring their own dishes for the gathering in lieu of that month's rent, the Iron Hand would pay for the lion's share of the food out of his own pocket. Even after eating supper herself, the smells wafting through the hall still had Elena's stomach growling again, and sent her passenger into a frenzy.

Elena hissed, clamping down hard on Sybil's arm and standing stock-still, back straight, chin up, eyes squeezed tight.

"Milady!" Sybil leaned in close, concern swelling in her voice. "Is it time—"

"N-no, no," Elena said, keeping a tight grip on her friend's arm. "It shall pass. Just... wait with me. Please." The pressure in her lower belly was immense, tight and firm and intensely uncomfortable, no matter how familiar she was with the sensation by that time. The world disappeared beyond her immediate periphery: the warm air, the heavy stone under her feet, Sybil's arm and panicked breathing, Elena's flared nostrils, and the tiny life pounding irritably at the walls of his fleshy prison.

It was an unwanted reminder of just how far along her pregnancy was, an admonition that eventually the happy moments and pleasurable distractions would end. A life was growing inside of her, one that would have to come out eventually—that was a frightening thing to consider all by itself, not to mention knowing she'd have to withstand pain like what she was experiencing at that moment. She took as many deep breaths as she could, all of the smells and scents filling her up, and waited for the pain to subside, pushing thoughts of labor, pain, blood and sorrow to the back of her mind.

The moment felt endless, but in time, the pressure subsided and died away. She felt a trickling of sweat at the nape of her neck, another trickling down between her breasts. Elena took a calming breath, eased her grip on Sybil's arm and opened her eyes again, finding a pair of steel-grey ones staring back at her, intense and so very large up close.

Elena gasped and rocked backwards, almost taking a step back as well. "Lord!" As to whether it was an oath or salutation, she'd let someone else decide.

Hugh Isarnon, the Iron Hand himself, had appeared out of thin air, it seemed. He was a tall man, broad-shouldered with wide hands to match. His hair was dark, nearly black, with streaks and spots of grey as befitting a man of his age. "Are you all right, starling?" he said, looking concerned.

For an instant, Elena nearly stuck out her chin and responded with a cool, dismissive response. Old habits were, it seemed, hard to break. Instead, Elena took a calming breath and smiled. "Quite all right, my Lord, my heart is glad at your returning. Your son simply finds his confinement less and less to his liking, I think." She took his hand, calloused and immense, in her own. "Just a momentary discomfort, is all." When the look on his face didn't change, she added, "I promise."

She felt the weight of his eyes, the intensity in his gaze as he watched her. There was a silent, imposing sort of beauty to him, a gentleness that warmed her heart when he was nearby. And yet, her husband could be an intimidating man—he had an air about him, a sometimes-overwhelming sense of presence, which had frightened Elena in her younger years. Even now, some unconscious part of her wanted to step back or turn away from his hard stare, until he smiled, squeezing her fingers in gentle affirmation. "As you say," he answered.

Elena huffed. "It *is* as I say, my Lord." She looked over Hugh's shoulder at his companion, a man even more immense and imposing than her husband. "Father Oswolf!"

The black-haired mountain of a Scot smiled, deliberately side-stepping around Hugh to embrace her. "'Tis good t'see ye, Milady." Elena had known Oswolf since she was a child, and she gladly returned the embrace. "An' you, Sybil, as well," he added.

"Welcome back, Father," Sybil said with a smile. The two looked at one another for a moment.

"Always a sight fer sore eyes y'are, Lady," Oswolf said next, turning back to Elena.

"It's hardly my eyes that are sore lately, Father," Elena said, deadpan.

"Och, dinnae worry yerself t'hard over that, dearie." He waved a hand in dismissal, the same gesture Elena herself had used just minutes ago. "The way I hear't, that sort o'thing'll work itself out in the right time, ye ken?"

"So Isolda—and everyone else, for that matter—keep telling me."

"Isolda?" Oswolf said, looking askance. "Yer... cook, aye?"

"And my midwife." Elena sniffed. "You'll have to excuse my poor state of dress, Father," she added, waving a hand at her garb in resignation after giving her husband a sidelong look. "I wasn't anticipating company until the morrow."

Oswolf pursed his lips and shook his head. "Think nothin' of't, lass."

"Done," she agreed, then turned her eyes back on her husband. "I'm *most* displeased with your arrival, my Lord. I didn't expect you to arrive back so soon."

The man blinked, his unspoken question written all over his big, beautiful face.

"Truly," she said, as though echoing back the very question he hadn't spoken aloud, yet one she'd heard as plainly as if he had. "I take it your early return means your investigation was successful?"

For a breath, Elena saw Hugh hesitate—it happened so fast she was sure anyone else might have missed it, but the telltale signs were there: the shift of his weight, the manner of how his eyes moved from side to side, the slightest pause before he opened his mouth to respond. There was a telling glance at Sybil, as though she was the source of his reluctance. When he did speak, his voice was low, quiet enough that only the four of them could hear it, "The Danes are starting to move again for the first time in nearly 30 years—there were attacks to the east at Rochester, Southampshire and Tanet, as far north as Chestershire: raiding parties, possibly in preparation of something... bigger."

Given Hugh's cautious tone of voice and the tight line of Oswolf's mouth, Elena felt a tremor of worry flutter somewhere beneath her heart. She said, "And if they were seen as close as Southampton—"

"Corfe could be next." Hugh nodded, pointing at Sybil. "You'll say nothing of this to anyone." His tone brooked no argument.

Sybil, her eyes slightly wide, shook her head quickly. "No, Milord," she answered, voice squeaking slightly.

The Lord nodded, satisfied, and looked back at Elena. "I think, my dear, we'll speak more of this soon enough."

It fell to Elena to break the awkward silence that followed. She squeezed her maidservant's arm in a wordless attempt to soothe the woman. "And now you've gone and spoiled my surprise." Knowing it was too late for such things, yet insisting on it anyway, Elena swept her free hand out to the entire hall around them.

Hugh's Hall had been decorated in shades of white, gold, green and more; long banners of dyed cloth stretched across the wooden beams overhead, bound at the corners with bluebells, yellow cowslips, and white wood blossoms with bright yellow centers. There were purple dog violets on long, green stems, cuckooflowers in bright pastel pinks, even woven garlands of tiny wild garlic. Elena had done much of that work herself, one of the few contributions she could make while resting in bed all day. Yet she'd insisted on going out to help oversee the picking of the flowers in person, even helping to pluck them herself when she could manage it—her back had been screaming at her ever since.

She waited a moment longer for both men to finish scanning the room and look back to her. "My Lord Husband approves, I hope," she said. Her tone was warm, if formal. In spite of his worrisome news, a tiny part of her still hoped he would be pleased, while a larger part worried he wouldn't. She looked up at him from under her raised eyebrows, steeling her heart for the disapproval that might come. Hugh was protective of her— sometimes a touch too much, in Elena's opinion, given how he insisted she stay in bed so much lately.

Hugh finished his appraisal of his Hall in studious silence, making a complete and full turn to take it all in. When he finished, he took her hand again and nodded again. "It will do, Wife." Elena felt a tightness in her chest begin to ease, gaining speed as she saw a small smile on his face. "It will do indeed," he said.

"Lovely work, t'be sure," Oswolf agreed. "An' whatever the good Isolda might b'cookin' in those kitchens o'hers, I'm a touch certain m'stomach's 'bout t'fill up jus' from the smell of't all." The humongous priest took a deep, hungry-sounding breath and sighed, patting both hands over his belly. "At least there's an end'n sight soon fer all this fastin' foolishness."

"But, Father," Sybil countered, "isn't the whole point of fasting to bring us nearer to God?"

"I s'pose't might, m'dear, Sybil, but..." Oswolf paused for a moment, looking over his shoulder out of some force of habit, it seemed to Elena, before turning back and answering in a softer voice. "I've known many a poor soul what could use a fuller belly t'bring 'imself closer t'God's glory... an' more'n a few Men o' the Cloth what could do wit' a few less meals fer t'same reason."

"Well said," Hugh answered in the same manner.

Elena looked from one man's face to the other, then back again. There was a long history between them, secrets she could never know or even begin to guess at, a life they'd lived in friendship together before she was even born. She had near-boundless affection for the unorthodox holy man, but still had to admit he was unlike any other priest she'd ever met. In truth, that was one of the reasons she liked him. Oswolf reminded her of Hugh, and in the months since her pregnancy's outset, Elena had come to treasure reminders of her husband more and more.

"Sybil."

"Yes, Milady?"

Elena was watching Hugh's face, the way his dark salt-and-pepper streaked hair caught the evening light, and she noticed his eyes looking at her, searching her face, taking measure of her. "Perhaps you and Father Oswolf might go check on Isolda and see just what she's working on this evening? I think... I think that it might be best if I went back to bed now." She pressed a hand on her stomach again, but the tremor in her belly had nothing to do with the unborn child sleeping fitfully within it. She still carried a lingering worry at her husband's earlier words, but his presence and watchful eyes were having a different effect on her, and not an unwelcome one.

Hugh, to his credit, only looked at his wife. Which was good, because if he'd shared some kind of look with Oswolf, Elena would have scratched out his eyes. Instead, Hugh offered his arm, and together they slowly turned and started towards the stairs again.

"I, ah, s'pose I'll b'seein' ylater, Milord?" Oswolf said. "Dinnae forget we've other matters t'speak of."

Hugh didn't look back, but nodded his head and grunted, waving a hand in some motion of affirmation as the Lord of the house led his Lady away.

A LOVING TOUCH

*E*lena enjoyed walking with Hugh, looking up at him, soaking in his presence, his warmth. It was enough to make her forget about her aching feet, and he let her lean on him for strength. But her heart was pounding by the time they reached their room—it was one of the only solitary bedrooms in the whole house, a luxury Elena was especially thankful to have, given how far into her pregnancy she was. Each new morning, she woke up wondering if that would be the day when the child would arrive, and each night came with a touch of disappointment.

Of course, disappointment was the furthest thing from her mind then, as she watched Hugh lock the door and hang the heavy key in its proper place. Something akin to butterflies fluttered about in her stomach, and she carefully took a seat on the edge of the bed, always mindful of her sore back. She had a dozen questions for him, all of which she swallowed down, ignoring the temptation to begin speaking right away. Elena didn't need to badger the man, she needed to have patience. She needed a distraction. And with company like Hugh Isarnon,

Elena had some definite ideas about ways to distract herself, fasts and abstinence be damned.

"Can she be trusted to keep quiet?" Hugh said.

"Who, Sybil?" Elena huffed, again waving her hand as if it was no matter. "I've known the woman for years. *You've* known her almost as long, Husband. She's loyal to a fault, and she'd sooner swallow her own teeth than willfully betray an order."

Hugh walked past the bed and over to the window, peering through the slender portal to the town in the distance. Elena had lived in Corfe her entire life, and like many of its inhabitants, rarely left its familiar environs; she could count the number of times on one hand. Hugh, by contrast, had traveled much of the length and width of England, even as far north as Scotland in his younger years, which was where he and Oswolf had met. Yet he inevitably returned to the place of his birth, drawn back by duty to the citizens who served him. Elena watched his face from over her shoulder—he seemed suddenly older to her, bearing a great weight she couldn't fathom or see.

Elena frowned, tilting her head to one side, watching him. "What's this all about, Husband? I haven't seen you this troubled since King Edgar died."

"I'm worried, starling," he said. It was a nickname he'd picked for her so many years ago and a familiar affectation, but his tone took the joy out of it. "The Danes, the sort of men who join these raiding parties... They come for plunder, for sport. They burn, they terrorize and they kill. And I'm told the English soldiers meant to protect those citizens from the Danes did the best they could, but I've heard once word reached Winchester, our young king and his advisers were... *displeased*." His lips pressed to a thin line. Whether intentionally or not, Hugh's face showed no emotion.

It'd been over two years since Elena and her husband had witnessed a royal coup, a tale so great and terrible it was hard to believe she'd even lived to see it, much less lived through it. After the early death of King Edgar, a man Hugh knew as a friend and loved as a brother for most of his life, the matter of succession was undecided between Edgar's progeny, two half-brothers: Edward, the elder son, and Æthelred, the younger. There was also the matter of dealing with Elfrida, Edgar's widow and mother of Æthelred, a cunning and conniving woman in her own right; Edward's mother had died when he was a boy, and Edward had idolized Elfrida beyond a point Elena ever claimed to understand.

"Well, I should certainly *hope* the citizens were protected," Elena said. "Who could be displeased by that?"

Hugh looked over at her for a moment, then turned his eyes back to the window. "It's my understanding that at Rochester, the town elders either sent a delegation out to meet the Danish boats, or they all but ordered the gates opened for the raiders to come in as they pleased, with the understanding that the loss of their treasure was a price well spent in the interest of avoiding any unnecessary hostilities. When the King's advisers heard this, they convinced him to send out a force to attack Rochester in retaliation."

"He gave the order to attack one of his own settlements?" Elena was stunned. "Why, in God's name, would he do *that*?"

The Lord rubbed his neck. "An object lesson, I presume: either give the Danes as good of a fight as possible, or the King's soldiers will show you what a good fight really looks like."

Elena snorted. "If that wasn't the boy-king's own idea—and it has a certain twisted, child's logic to it, I'll warrant—it sounds as vindictive and shallow-minded as anything the Queen Regent could conjure up instead. Idiots."

When the matter of deciding which of Edgar's sons should be the new king, Elfrida had believed her son Æthelred was the best choice. The rub of it was Hugh had supported Edward's right to be king at first, but he soon came to regret that choice when the young man tried to force himself on Elena, and then beat her for refusing him; Elena still carried the scars of that beating on her back, and they ached terribly on days threatened by heavy rain. By the time Hugh tried to change his mind and go over to Æthelred's camp, it was too late, and Edward became the next king.

A plot was hatched then, one whose terrible culmination transpired just a short distance from their bedroom, when men loyal to Æthelred—and, foremost of all, Elfrida—murdered Edward in the yard of Hugh's Hall. Elfrida—now the Queen Regent, the power behind King Æthelred's throne and, likely as not, the most powerful person in the whole kingdom—still remembered Hugh's betrayal of her son. Elfrida was known for many things, but forgiveness wasn't one of them.

"Our people..." Hugh sighed after his voice faded away, rubbing at his face with one hand in consternation. "The men here are strong and stout-hearted, but they know little of war and bloodshed. There haven't been more than a score's worth of men of fighting stock in Dorsetshire since my grandfather was a boy. Not enough to defend the whole town, anyway."

It took more effort than she wanted to admit, but Elena managed to stand again, smothering any grunts of discomfort. When she walked up behind her husband, she slid her hands up his back: Hugh Isarnon was taller than she by more than a foot and outweighed her by nearly ten stone, but that made him solid, like the stone wall he was leaning against. It comforted her to touch him, and she turned her face to press her cheek against him, curling her arms about his waist. "Yet, fighting stock or no, you shall lead them bravely, if you must... and I believe they will follow, faithfully." When Hugh turned around, she kept her arms close to him, pressing herself to his chest as best she could with the massive swell of her belly. Turning her head up, chin to his chest, Elena forced a tiny smile for his benefit. "You are a good man, Hugh. Everyone in Corfe knows it. You will do what you must for your people, and they will do what they must for their Lord in turn."

The Iron Hand smiled—it was sad at the edges, but Elena saw more joy in it than pain. He touched her face and she closed her eyes, pressing into his caress. "Am I truly so good as that, Elena?" he said.

"And even more-so," she answered, opening her eyes to look at his. "I've seen more of that than anyone. Perhaps, if God is fortunate, the Danes shan't come. But," she took a deep breath, "if they do, I shall pray for your success, and survival, and even stand next to you myself to fight them back, if I must."

Hugh laughed, but it lacked the mocking bite she half-expected, so she kept her calm. "Perish the thought, starling. If I were to sic you on the Danes, not a one of them would survive the meeting, and I can hardly call myself Lord if my Lady does all of the fighting for me, can I?"

Elena smirked up at him. "Husband, there are some days of late where I can barely stand up straight. I'd hardly call myself the intimidating sort... unless Danes happen to quake in fear at short, pregnant, English women."

"What I wouldn't give to see that." Hugh bent down and pressed a long, loving kiss to her mouth. The first was tender, but the one after it was warmer and went right through Elena, all the way down to her toes.

"What *else* would you like to see, my Lord?" she asked, a breathless murmur as she cupped his face in her hands. Elena's heart was full and aching with love for her husband, and from the look on his face, he felt much the same way.

"Well, perhaps if we did something about that gown of yours, you might show me a few things," he said, kissing up the bridge of her nose.

"'Did something,' hmm?" Elena reached up to her neck and began to unfasten the knotted string holding the nightgown in place. "I was under the impression my wifely duties were to be withheld until tomorrow morning, my Lord."

"I don't remember agreeing to anything of the sort," he answered in a playful growl. "I've had you on my mind for the better part of a week now, starling. I'm not sure God Himself could withhold you from me now."

"Heathen." Elena smiled and let the gown slip from her fingers, slither down her body and over her round belly before it collapsed in a round pool of pale fabric on the woven rug at her feet. "Will you tend to me, my love?" she whispered, standing pale, naked and unashamed before his greedy eyes.

"Gladly," he said. Elena noticed, more and more of late, she found herself stripped to the skin when he hadn't so much as removed a thread of clothing, but the feel of his thick, callused fingers and warm hands on her flesh were one reason she never complained. He touched her everywhere when he bent to kiss her again, sliding his hands over her shoulders, up her slender neck, down her back and over the swell of her bottom—the last received a firm squeeze, which made her moan into his mouth, swiping her tongue across his lips as she pulled away from the kiss.

Once upon a time, he would've ordered her, and Elena would have fought or resisted him. Now, she willingly and even happily turned on her heel on the woven rug next to their box-shaped bed, bending at her waist to place her hands atop the coverlet. Her belly, heavy with child, swung low until it brushed the blankets; her breasts, heaving and swollen, hung down like ripened apples that would overfill her hands if she held them. This was Elena's first pregnancy and though it had its downsides she could do without—aches and pains that left her in poor spirits and lacking in proper sleep—some parts of it were absolutely divine. Her sense of smell was sharper, her plain appearance had improved, her body becoming curvy and more pleasant to look at, she thought; her mouse-brown hair had thickened and developed curls. She felt attractive, even pretty. And there was Hugh's desire of her, which only seemed to gain in strength and vigor as her body continued to change.

Elena could feel him just behind her and to one side, like he was radiating heat and desire, which she soaked up into her very skin. He brushed his fingers up from her thigh, over her bottom, and back down again. The touch was whisper-faint, and she shivered with delight, perverse thought it might have been.

"I missed you," he said. She could hear rustling, a nameless sound she, nevertheless, recognized. "I missed... this."

"And I, you," she said, turning her head towards the sound of his voice, but her eyes were closed. The sensation of his touch, the allure of her desire for him, it was stronger when her eyes were closed, she'd noticed. "Now... please," she added, in a whisper. There was nothing else she had to add—they both knew what she meant.

The feel of his leather belt, wide and flat, connected to her upraised backside. Elena bowed her sore back, thrust herself back and widened her stance—her mouth opened wider, teeth pressed together as she hissed. It hurt, of course, but the pain was a necessary evil, for what came *after* the pain was worth the asking price. As the strikes continued, she smelled her arousal, sensed the fire in her wide belly, a contrasting warmth to the bright, white heat spreading across her ass. Soon Elena had to ease down onto her elbows, crossing them, clutching the blanket tight as the bed bore more of her weight. The blankets rubbed at her swollen nipples, swirled around her stomach, her legs shook at each blow, but now the pain was secondary to her desire, hotter still than anything his belt or hand could do to her.

Hugh paused his spanking for a moment, drawing his fingertips up between her thighs. The sensation of his touch made her whimper. When he reached her center, coated his touch in the liquid proof of her lust, slid a finger inside of her, she pressed her face into the bed and moaned as loud and hard as any whore would have. That was the effect Hugh Isarnon had on her, the hold he had over her—he could turn her from the most proper woman into a rutting harlot in minutes, and most times, she went willingly along with it.

There was no warning, no time to prepare herself. When he grabbed her hip with one hand, Elena gasped; when she felt the tip of his manhood nuzzling against her tender, swollen mound, Elena whimpered; when he entered her in a single push, Elena called out to him. Pressing her forehead into the bed, she looked back with drowsy, heavy-lidded eyes, catching sight of his body, and how he was still fully dressed. But it was his face she focused on, a tight, tense mask of effort, as though he couldn't wait for a moment longer before he had to have her. That was the effect *she* had over Hugh Isarnon—willingly giving him access to her body often led him to please her even sooner than he would have if she'd asked for it.

Elena smiled with satisfaction as she braced herself on the bed. The pounding thrusts began a second later, and then it was hard to brace herself at all, given how insistent his movements were. Elena's breathing quickened through flared nostrils and curved lips. The feeling of being completely and totally *full* was beyond description, as if her entire body became an extension of something beyond her control. Elena's consciousness seemed to want to float away, anchored only by the clutching fingernails in the blankets and the invading flesh pounding between her legs.

The way he took her was so rough, so simple and full of need. When his thrusts became quicker and more desperate, she squeezed the blankets tighter and prepared for the end, beckoning her quivering legs to hold up just a few moments longer.

"Please," she said again, this time in a weak-sounding whimper. Elena heard the catch of his breath as her plea broke him, and hid a smile into the crook of her arm when he came, with all of its usual hallmarks: spasming flesh, the feeling of his seed spilling over, the clutch of his fingertips in her flesh so tight she was liable to bruise from it. Elena held her breath for a second—Isolda, her midwife, said sometimes coitus could wake the child in her belly, urging the birthing process to begin... but nothing happened. After a long moment, she took a new breath while slowly rolling to her side on the bed, easing off of his softening flesh.

Elena was reminded of their first months and years together, when sex was just a physical act. For more than ten years, she'd simply been the Lady of the house, following her Lord Husband's commands, warming his bed and servicing his lust when it suited him. The difference now was her heart was full of love and desire for *him*—for the man he was, the partner who loved and desired her in return.

Continuing the roll and ending up on her back, Elena took a moment to stretch, raising her arms high over her head in a feline sort of motion. Hugh stood half-bent, catching his breath, still dressed, aside from the pair of trousers dangling at his knees. The look of it was so comical she started laughing before she could stop herself, and tried to smother it behind one hand.

Hugh raised his head, looking at her with surprise. "What is it?"

Managing to repress her laughter into something closer to a coughing chuckle, Elena pillowed her head on both arms and smiled up at him. "Begging your pardon, my Lord, but... you look ridiculous, quite frankly."

He looked down at himself and back up to her again, a self-conscious smirk on his face. "Do I now?"

"Quite, my Lord," she answered, resting one hand atop her round belly. "Methinks you might consider ridding yourself of those useless clothes and get into bed. You've a wife who requires more tending to, after all."

"Does she," he said, in the same tone as before. Licking his lips, Hugh began to kick off his boots. "Perhaps I'll attend to that now, then—assuming she's interested in my company, of course."

She was interested, and Elena saw to it her husband was appraised of just *how* interested as the evening wore on.

A HAND FORCED

*T*he next day's festivities would begin in earnest at Midday. Sybil woke Elena up just after dawn, same as always, but the Lady's current state meant that most of the preparations and work had to be done by others, leaving her as a glorified overseer, and seeing as that was Sybil's job anyhow, it left Elena without much to do. To that end, the Lord and Lady met with Father Oswolf in a small sitting room off of the main hall where they could talk more privately. There was a foul taste in her mouth that morning—Hugh's fault, although she'd never have admitted it—so she sat and sipped at a warm cup of diluted small ale, a very weak alcoholic beverage made by her husband's own brewer. She'd never cared for such drinks until her pregnancy, but lately the weak, mild taste of it agreed with her.

"There's nothin' for't, Milord," Oswolf said, shaking his head. "Ye'll get no help from Winchester, whether ye petition the King or go yerself t'grovel at 'is feet proper-like—no doubt jus' the sorta look the Queen would like best, lettin' the whole o'the royal court watch the Iron Hand 'imself beg Æthelred fer table scraps."

"Then what do you propose I do, Os?" Hugh leaned back, a

foul look on his face. "Offer my people refuge in my Hall while the Danes pick the town clean? Or perhaps I'll ask the barbarous horde nicely to turn around when they make it to shore?"

"There's still as much a chance they may not come to these shores at all, my Lord," Elena pointed out.

"Aye," Oswolf said, nodding with a touch of reluctance. "Ye may trust t'Providence, t'be sure. But—"

"'A simple man trusts, a wiser one acts,'" Hugh said. It had the sound of a saying in it, one that Elena hadn't heard before.

The Scottish priest nodded in agreement, saying nothing further.

"And there's something else," Hugh said, "something I haven't spoken of yet. To either of you."

Oswolf looked intrigued. Elena sat a little straighter in her seat—or as straight as someone with a belly of such size could manage. "My Lord?"

"The news I got from the attack on Tanet—it was said the Danish ships were flying Norman colors."

"God's breath," Oswolf said, sounding like an oath. "Yer man was sure of't?"

"And confirmed by two more who also witnessed the battle," Hugh said, nodding. "I don't have to remind you Normandy just happens to sit on the other side of the South Sea from where we now sit," he added, face grim. "That we haven't been attacked already might be proof of Providence, but I don't intend to trust that for much longer."

There was a long moment of uncomfortable silence between the three of them. Elena finished off her drink but didn't have the heart to put the cup aside, as if so small a sound might still disrupt her husband's thinking.

And yet, it was Hugh who spoke first. "If the Normans are helping the Danes attack towns along our coastline, that might be enough to force Æthelred's hand—he would have to marshal forces to man the fort at Wareham, north of us. Corfe is close enough to fall under its protection, and they'd be duty-bound to answer if we called for aid."

"Aye," Oswolf said, "fer all the good it did at Southampton—the force at the fort there didnae have much luck protectin' the town, from what I heard."

Hugh pressed his lips together, nodding once, not answering.

Elena looked from one man, to the other, then back again. "But... I thought the two of you went off on your journey together. Was that not the case?"

"Nay, lass," Oswolf said. "Four ears an' eyes can do twice the work o'two, iffin' ye follow me."

"Well enough, I suppose." Turning the cup over in her hands, she cleared her throat. "Father, you said you needed to speak to my husband about something else. Should I excuse myself?"

"Mm?" The priest seemed puzzled for a split second. "Did I?"

"Last night, before we retired for the evening," Elena said. She was too practiced by that time to show a hint of a blush, anything which would've implied she and Hugh had done anything more than gone immediately to bed. Which they had done, but the other details were best left unsaid—Elena *was* a proper Lady, after all.

"Oh, that!" Oswolf snapped his fingers. "Nay, Milady, ye need do no such thing." He hesitated for a long moment, searching for the right words, before he continued. "Pish-post, I'll just b'out wit't. Matter o'fact—"

There was a light knocking at the door, sudden enough to cut off the priest in mid-stream. Hugh sat up straighter. "Enter," he said.

The door opened, and Sybil appeared. She looked at Oswolf first—Elena wondered about that for a moment—then made the perfunctory bow to both heads of the house. "Beg pardon for the interruption, Milord, but there's a guest here to see you."

From the look on Hugh's face, Elena guessed he hadn't been expecting a visitor. "Anyone I would know, Sybil?" he asked.

Sybil's eyes went a little wide, and she shook her head. "Oh no, Milord, I shouldn't think so. He's, ah..." The maidservant paused for a split second. "Well, I think it's safe to say he's not from anywhere in Dorsetshire that I'm familiar with. Shall I send him away?"

Hugh and Elena shared a look. Something unsaid passed between them—Hugh gave a faint shrug, then pushed to his feet before offering his wife a hand to help her stand. "Father, perhaps you'll accompany us?" he said.

"Surely, Milord," Oswolf answered as he stood. Elena was comforted by the thought of her husband having Oswolf to watch his back. Holy man or not, Oswolf wasn't someone she would have wanted to get on the bad side of. "Shall we?" he said.

The main hall was full of scents: from the plucked flowers, from the food Isolda and her staff were setting out on the lord's table, from the warm spring breezes blowing in through the open doors. There were platters of roasted meat, steamed and roasted vegetables, and open casks of fermented drinks so strong her eyes watered as they passed by. Servants and early guests were everywhere, all dressed in their festival finery, such a garish collection of colors it made Elena's eyes want to cross. There was a tumult of activity, and a loud cacophony of sounds ringing in her ears from dozens of conversations happening all at once. Hugh and Oswolf towered head and shoulders over everyone else, and Elena was used to being the short one, so having her husband to lean on made it easier to pass through the crowd. Sybil led the way, walking out through the tall doors and out into the front yard.

Hugh's Hall was the largest of several structures that encompassed Lord Isarnon's estate—a main hall built of stone, rather than timber; stables for the Lord's livestock and horses; and other smaller buildings like the brewery, storehouse, and more. They were surrounded by walls of wooden stakes, providing a rudimentary defense if ever needed. The entire walled structure sat tucked in tight inside of a gap in a long line of chalk-colored hills, with gated openings to both the north and the south.

The southern gates were opened wide, and a man sat on horseback just inside of them. His reins were loose in one hand, while he leaned backwards on the other, balanced on the beast's rump while looking around, appearing to be completely at his leisure. His hair was blond, tied back from his face in a topknot; his matching beard, which was substantial in size, hung down to his chest, interwoven with wooden beads and what looked like short bits of bone or ivory. He also had two swords in his belt— from the look of his physique, he knew how to use them. The most notable marking on him was a black stripe, a tattoo of some kind, encircling his neck on both sides.

The man was a Dane; he stuck out like a weed in a field full of English flowers. Two men armed with pikes, two of Hugh's men—who at times seemed almost invisible, given how little Elena sometimes noticed their presence—stood on either side of the gate, looking cautious at the rider's appearance.

"Ho, Lord Isarnon," the rider said to Hugh, raising a hand, palm out. "Father, Milady," he added, nodding his head to Oswolf and Elena in turn.

"Ho, rider," Hugh said, nodding his head back. "You come alone?"

The blond rider looked back over his shoulder at the empty road leading from the Hall to Corfe, then back. The smile on his face came easy to him, Elena thought. "Seems that I have. You *are* the Iron Hand, aren't you?"

Hugh nodded again. "I am. Who are you?"

"Ivan Black-Neck, here on behalf of Ealdorman Elfhar of Mercia."

Elena felt Hugh go stiff at the ealdorman's name.

Ivan looked around the yard once more, then back to Hugh. "Will you offer me safe passage to your Hall?"

Hugh seemed to ponder it for a moment, then nodded a third

time, beckoning. "Granted." The Lord's invitation meant the rider had Hugh's protection, and would be completely safe while he lingered within the Lord's house.

As Ivan slid out of the saddle, a young boy of seven or eight ran across the yard from the stables. After one of the pike-armed soldiers took possession of the man's two swords, the boy—one of Gerald's sons, whose name escaped her—took the horse and pulled it back towards the stables.

Now horseless and relieved of his weapons, the top-knotted man approached. He wore a leather vest over his shirt, and pants to match, both dyed dark brown with colored beads interwoven with leather laces. He wore several metal rings on each hand, and a silver ornament of some kind on a leather string hanging from his neck: an upside-down, T-shaped hammer—it was a sigil of Thor, one of the pagan gods that some of the Danes worshiped.

"My wife, Elena," Hugh said, motioning to her first, "and Father Oswolf, a priest of our church here."

Oswolf and Ivan took a brief second to size each other up. Hugh and Oswolf were both taller than Ivan, but Ivan was likely to be the more seasoned soldier.

"I offer premature congratulations to you both, then," Ivan said, looking down at Elena's swollen stomach before dipping his head deeper in a show of respect.

"Thank you," Elena said. Hugh seemed to be cautiously welcoming to the stranger, so she resolved to do the same. "Have you come far to reach our house?"

"Far enough, I suppose," Ivan answered with a shrug. "From the look of things, you've quite a gathering planned."

"'Tis Easter Sunday, Milord," Oswolf said. "One'f our holier feastdays, ye ken."

"Ah yes." Ivan nodded. "I'm familiar with the custom. Lord Elfhar is an observant man of your Church, he's informed me of some particulars of the day."

"This way, then," Hugh said, and led the way back into the house, Elena walking next to him. Ivan followed, with Oswolf right behind him. It felt to her more like escorting a prisoner than a guest.

"Are you all right?" she whispered, leaning in closer, holding onto her husband's arm as they walked. "Is it safe to have him here?"

"Safe enough," he answered, whispering as well. "Keep your ears open, starling."

They returned to the same sitting room, but now with a certain air of ceremony about them. Word passed through the Hall quickly that a guest had arrived, so Elena was saved from having to order anyone around. A mug of ale was brought for Ivan, who sampled it, declared it more than satisfactory and drank until his cup was empty, bits of foam staining his mustache before he licked it clean.

The three men sat at the table—Hugh at the head, Ivan and Oswolf opposite one another. Elena sat behind Hugh, hands folded across her belly, remaining quiet but listening intently as her husband had requested.

Ivan nodded his head to Elena. "Is it customary to talk with women present, Lord?"

Hugh nodded, offering no explanation. "Speak."

The Dane looked at Elena for a second, then shrugged. "It matters not; I was told the matter would concern her as well."

Elena perked up a little at that, curiosity bubbling up in her belly.

Ivan leaned on his elbows, slowly turning the empty cup in his ringed fingers. "I come on behalf of my Master, Ealdorman Elfhar. He seeks a boon from you on a matter of great importance, or so he tells me."

The Iron Hand was quiet for a moment. "Of what kind?"

"I can only speak as to what my Lord has seen fit to inform me, you understand," Ivan said.

Again, Hugh nodded, not answering.

"He told me of a young English king who was slain in these parts several years ago. I was told the deed was done in secret, some sort of conspiracy to put the young Æthelred on the throne—the particulars of that don't concern me, Lord, so rest easy." Ivan was taking a bit of a risk, or so it seemed to Elena. From his casual, cautious tone, it almost seemed like Ivan supposed that Hugh was involved in the plot on Edward's life. Glancing to one side, she saw Oswolf's face, the surprise in the man's widened eyes.

Ivan continued, "My Lord understands his body might be somewhere close-by, that you and your wife might know where his resting place can be located."

The air became tense, almost stifling. All three men were silent for a long moment.

"An'...jus' where, exactly, did yer Lord happen t'discover this information?" Oswolf asked, leaning across the table, palms flat.

Ivan smiled and shrugged one shoulder. "He didn't say, Father. If Lord Hugh thinks my Master's information is false, then I'll thank him for his ale and be on my way." The blond Dane looked back at Hugh again. "What say you, Lord?"

Hugh was quiet for a moment longer. Elena watched him sit as still as if he'd been turned to stone, but that was his way— Hugh was thinking, considering his options, contemplating just what to say. She knew the signs well. It wasn't her place to speak up until he did, or until he gave her permission to do so, so Elena stayed quiet for now.

"What does he want to do with it?" Hugh said after a time.

"I suppose he means to bury the body elsewhere, Lord," Ivan said. "I'm merely the man's messenger, so that's an assumption on my part, granted. I was told he supported Æthelred's right to the throne over Edward, but it seems to me my Lord carries some regret at how badly it ended for the elder brother when it was all over."

"Iffin' memory serves me right," Oswolf said, "Lord Elfhar made quite a name fer 'imself durin' Edward's reign—much o'the Church's land changed hands. After't was all said'n done, Elfhar was left holdin' the rights fer quite a bit o'real estate—a princely sum, even."

"I'm only a hired sword-hand, Father," Ivan said, "but if I was freer with my tongue... I'd be inclined to agree with you." The Dane showed off that easy smile of his and didn't comment further.

Hugh sat up, and clapped his hands loudly together. "I'd like to speak with my wife and the Father in private." When Sybil, standing close-by as always, opened the door, Hugh told her, "Take this man to the kitchens and give him whatever he asks to eat." To Ivan, he said, "I'll summon you back soon to give my answer."

"My thanks, Lord," Ivan said, pushing to his feet. Elena saw Sybil's eyes widen slightly again when Ivan fixed his eyes on her, but the maidservant bobbed a quick curtsy in answer to her lord's order and ushered Ivan out of the room, shutting the door behind them.

Hugh stretched out one hand behind him. Elena pulled her chair closer, taking it without him having to ask.

Oswolf, still staring at the door, scrubbed at one cheek. "Ye dinnae s'pose he came as part o'some grander plot t'do any harm, d'ye?"

"It's possible," Hugh answered with a shrug. "I know Elfhar —this has the feel of him in it, somehow. He has almost as much influence as Æthelred himself; they call him '*Princeps Merciorium Gentis*'—Prince of the Mercian people. He was loyal to Edgar when the King was alive. Now he's older and wiser than most, and he's not the kind to dance on Elfrida's strings just because she wishes it. If this is some kind of trick, I don't see it yet."

"So you think Ivan is telling the truth?" Elena asked.

"As much as he knows, I suppose," Hugh said. The Lord looked over to Oswolf next. "What say you?"

"I suspect the man'f more'n what 'e says, but I s'pose I do that'f ev'ryone t'ese days," Oswolf said, sounding tired. The priest's brogue got thicker and harder to make out when he was lacking sleep, Elena noticed. "But, I believe he tells't true, Hugh. Archbishop Dunstan sent me t'see ye fer the same reason."

Hugh blinked. "So... the 'other matters' you mentioned us needing to speak of were about that?"

Oswolf hesitated for a brief moment, then nodded. "Aye. I didnae rush the matter, seein' as nobody outside'f this room e'en knows where the body lies at the moment, an' t'ain't likely that the young man's bones'll jus' dig 'emselves out anytime soon." Oswolf spread his hands in a helpless gesture. "I was jus' about t'broach the subject when this Black-Neck fellow happened along, an'...well, 'ere we are, then."

"And there wasn't anything *else* you wanted to talk about, Os?" Hugh said, raising an eyebrow.

The brutish Scot cleared his throat, as though suddenly uncomfortable.

Elena was too focused on the subject of Edward to pay much attention to Oswolf's discomfort. "But what does the Archbishop want with Edward's body?" she said. "Or is he, too, suffering from a guilty conscience, same as Lord Elfhar?"

Oswolf's smile was thin, as mirthless as a scar. "Nay, lass. Worse. There's already talk'f canonizin' the lad—'Edward t'Martyr,' they're callin' 'im."

"Edward, a *saint*? Wh-why that's..." Elena was half out of her chair, clutching the arms with trembling fingers. "That's preposterous!" She didn't even notice Hugh had gotten up until she felt his hands on her shoulders, heard him gently shushing her as he eased her down into her chair again. She was panting hard all of a sudden. "That man... *beat* me. He tore off my dress and... and *whipped* me... like some kind of *animal*." Elena trembled all over, and when she felt Hugh's hands squeezing her shoulders tighter, she bit her lip to keep from continuing further.

Oswolf spread his hands again. "As Master Ivan said, lass, I'm naught but the messenger. Dinnae blame me fer Dunstan's scheming, ye ken?" The priest looked up at Hugh, sounding contrite, even apologetic. "Yer a smart man, Milord, but I dinnae see a way t'wiggle outta this one—iffin' ye deny Elfhar's request, rest assured Dunstan won't be s'easily denied. Iffin' I know the man, he'll see fit t'order yer acquiescence wit' all the authority the Church gives 'im. By hook'r crook, Edward's body *will* be found an' re-interred elsewhere, an' they mean t'force yer hand t'get what they want." Oswolf looked back at her. "M'sorry, Elena."

AN UNEXPECTED JOURNEY

*E*lena was in such a state afterwards that Hugh insisted she go back to their room and rest. One part of her wanted to argue just on principle's sake, but a much, much larger part didn't want to be around to witness whatever discussion there was surrounding the dead King Edward, because she wasn't sure she could control her temper—just the memory of the man was enough to set her blood to boiling.

After Hugh tucked her in bed, Elena waited for him to shut the door before she got right back up again. She didn't follow, but instead rolled onto her feet with a grimace and a grunt of discomfort as she went to draw the curtains—she wanted privacy, to be alone with her thoughts, however unpleasant they were. Already she could hear the hum of voices in the distance, floating through Hugh's Hall, as the festivities were starting and more guests began to arrive. People from the town and all over the county would visit, filling the Hall to capacity, spilling out into the yard and beyond. Meanwhile, all Elena wanted to do was bury herself in her blankets and sulk.

Once the curtains were pulled, she felt the tiniest bit better. Due to the warmer weather, most of the tapestries or embroideries that covered the walls in wintertime had been removed, leaving the room mostly bare, save for a couple of oak chests she and Hugh shared for their belongings, a table and pair of small benches for seating, and the bed. That bed was a reminder of Hugh, and as she lay down again, Elena pressed her nose into his side of the bed, into his pillow, breathing in the scent of him. Her husband could keep the demons in her mind at bay for a time. She wished he was there with her, or she was still sitting with him, keeping his counsel, trying to help in whatever small way she could. A woman's place wasn't to be seen or heard unless it was wished of her, but Hugh often *did* wish it. It felt like she was failing him, allowing her emotions about Edward to cloud her judgment and common sense.

But when Elena reached over her shoulder, she could feel one of her old scars, the skin grown tough and textured like old leather from the horsewhip that Edward had beat her with. It was a mercy someone with a temper like that hadn't reigned as king for very long, and she remembered feeling happy after he was dead, no matter how wrong that was—happy someone had done the deed she could've never done on her own. The idea of anyone venerating him as a martyr turned her stomach.

Time passed. Elena dozed, alone with her thoughts, alone in the bed she wished Hugh could be lying in with her. However long she slept, she was instantly awake again when she heard a loud knocking at the bedroom door. "Milady?" More knocking. "Lady Elena, it's Isolda."

Elena rolled out of bed and went to open the door. "Yes?" She meant to say more, but when she saw who was waiting for her, she stopped. Isolda was there—the woman was almost old enough to be Elena's mother, her brown hair touched with grey at the temples and in long streaks across her scalp. She had a hard face and didn't smile often, but her bright, blue eyes were comforting in their own way. Standing behind Isolda was Hugh, hands folded behind his back, saying nothing.

"Is everything all right?" Elena said, looking from Hugh, to her midwife, and back again.

"His Lordship asked that I give you a thorough checking over." Isolda gave Hugh an open look of disapproval over her shoulder.

"But, I don't—"

"Elena." When Hugh spoke her name, she stopped. The look on his face was equally puzzling and troubling, and it seemed best to ignore her usual temptation for arguing. Instead, she stepped back, opening the door wider to let them both in.

Isolda entered first, still with the displeased look on her face. "Begging the Lord's pardon, but do you really need to be present for this? A new mother's entitled to some bit of privacy, whether the child's arrived yet or not."

"I won't be a distraction," he said, taking a seat near the head of the bed, his back to the wall.

The two women looked at one another, and it seemed that Isolda either wanted Elena to object, or wanted to object more on the Lady's behalf and couldn't. Elena shook her head softly, and made her way back to the bed, taking Hugh's hand before she sat down.

The midwife pressed her lips to a thin line, blew out a sharp breath through her nostrils and nodded. "Let's get to it, then. Lie down, Milady, if you would." Once her complaints were aired, Isolda was all business, she slid Elena's gown up and over the round hump of her belly, then began applying gentle pressure against a number of spots, checking the baby's position, confirming his head was still down and in the right place. "Has there been any pain?"

"Only everywhere and all the time," Elena said, grumbling.

Isolda closed her eyes, blew out a breath, then showed a rare smile. "Any sort of unfamiliar pain, Milady?"

Elena shook her head. "No, nothing like that." As the examination continued, she looked back at Hugh. "Did you tell the man you'd accept Elfhar's request?"

"Mm," Hugh grunted, and nodded in the affirmative. "No use fighting the inevitable. Black-Neck's already gone, off to report the news to his Master—and I expect it won't be long before Dunstan hears the news, as well."

"Well, *that*—" Elena was cut off when an especially hard push from Isolda's fingers against her ribs made her breath catch, and an unwelcomed kick from the baby in the same spot made her grunt in protest. "Isolda!"

"He's in the proper place, at least," Isolda said, ignoring Elena's protest. "I think it best that you not undergo a more thorough examination, given the circumstances." The older woman scowled at Hugh. "But I expect that, barring any... *unforeseen* emergencies," another scowl and sigh followed, "everything will be in order to deliver once you return."

The word *deliver* made Elena's stomach begin to drop, but a very different word grabbed her attention instead. "Return?" She blinked, then looked back at Hugh again as she pulled her gown down.

Hugh nodded. "I need you to go with me, starling."

"Go with... You want to leave? Now?" She sat up, jaw falling open. "Are you serious?"

"Quite." The Lord nodded again. "That's why I asked Isolda to check if it was safe for you to ride today."

"Safe?" Isolda snorted. "Begging the Lord's pardon *again,* but of *course* it isn't safe. She's a mother-to-be, Milord, and may I heavily stress the '*to-be*' part of my statement. She should be resting in bed, not galloping off on some wild adventure when she's liable to go into labor at any time." Isolda looked at Elena. "What did my mother do, Milady? She warned me not to marry a horseman, she did. And did I listen? Of course not. And what happened? My Edith happened, that's what."

Elena wracked her brain. "Edith is your... second child?"

Isolda nodded. "It's the smell of horseflesh, I'm sure of it. Just a whiff of the stuff sent Edith into such a kicking fit I don't think I slept a wink for my whole last month of pregnancy." The midwife looked up at her Lord again, shaking her head. "It's bad luck, Milord."

"It's only three or four miles," Hugh said, taking Isolda's scolding in stride. "I wouldn't insist if I didn't think it was necessary." He only had eyes for Elena, though, who thought her husband looked both sad and resolute at the same time. "It's something she has to do. That *we* have to do."

"Shall I fetch Sybil?" Isolda said.

"No. The less people we take with us, the faster we'll return, and I want Elena back here before nightfall. Help your Lady get dressed—the horses are waiting. Elfhar and Dunstan will be meeting us at Wareham." And with that, he stood, kissed Elena's knuckles, and stepped out of the bedroom, shutting the door behind him.

The women looked at one another for a moment. Elena pushed to her feet all the same, pulling the gown up and over her head, throwing it onto the bed without a hint of shame or hesitation. Isolda didn't shrink back or hide her eyes—at that point, she'd seen Elena undressed more than once.

"I suppose that's that, then," Elena said. "If I must go..." She bit her lip and shrugged, hoping her concern wasn't showing.

"Just be careful," Isolda warned, already on her knees in front of one of the wooden chests. "You'll be neither the first nor last woman to injure yourself or the babe if you push yourself or the horse too hard. The hills are gentle enough from here to Wareham, so that's a small mercy, I suppose." Isolda began pulling out one of her Lady's dresses and other garments.

"Not that one, Isolda; the green one would be better. It's more comfortable."

"I'd feel better if you weren't all alone on the road, unattended to except for a couple of… *men*," Isolda said with a snort as she helped Elena pull the dress over her head.

"I'd insist on asking Sybil to come along, but you heard my husband. And there's too much going on with today's festivities," Elena said, falling back into her matronly habits like pulling on a pair of old, sheepskin gloves. "Just stick close to her—she'll need whatever help you can give her. Once she hears my Lord is taking me off to Wareham, of all places, she'll be liable to consider stealing a horse and riding off after us."

Isolda showed off another one of her rare smiles. "Well, what she isn't told won't hurt her, will it, Milady?"

HUGH AND OSWOLF were waiting outside, and the priest was already in the saddle as the Lady of the house waddled out the doors, leaning on Isolda for support; it seemed to her Oswolf was disappointed at seeing Elena, although that might've just been her imagination. She'd lost count of the offered well wishes and belly rubs offered by the numerous houseguests, and by the time she reached the grey-haired mount that was saddled and waiting for her, Elena Isarnon was downright cranky. "If someone else touches me, I may scream," she growled, baring her teeth like a dog.

The priest raised both hands in a show of surrender, but Hugh stepped to her side of the mare, offering a hand to her—he did *not* take her hand on his own accord, which was probably the only reason she let him touch her at all. Grumbling under her breath, Elena took hold of the saddle with her empty hand, permitted him to raise her foot the rest of the way to slide it into the stirrup, then helped her over the top of the horse until she found a comfortable enough spot to sit. In truth, *all* of it was uncomfortable, but she smothered any further complaints and grabbed the reins in both hands, deciding the only recourse she had left was to wait for the whole affair to be over with.

"Remember what I told you," Isolda said.

Elena nodded.

"We'll be back by this evening," Hugh said as he climbed into the saddle himself. "Have our room prepared to make your Mistress comfortable upon our return, if you would."

"Of course, Milord."

Hugh clicked his tongue, nudging his steed to start moving. Elena and Oswolf followed. The great roan carrying the priest was so big she was sure it had to be twice the size of her tiny mare, but the larger beast was remarkably well-behaved and permitted Elena to pass ahead without complaint. She noted, in passing, that both of the men with her were armed. Hugh had a sword buckled at his waist, while Oswolf had a stout, heavy-looking cudgel and staff both tucked into the straps of his saddle. Riding off unescorted, even in Hugh's own lands, wasn't a task meant to be undertaken lightly, or without some protection.

They left Hugh's Hall and Corfe behind, taking the northern exit and the road that led to their destination. Elena couldn't manage even a trot for more than a few moments before she was visibly bothered by the pain of all the jostling, so Hugh immediately slowed their pace back down to a walk. That was a little easier to bear, and aside from the discomfort caused by the saddle itself, Elena managed as well as could be expected.

"I'd forgotten how free Isolda's tongue could be, my Lord," she said later.

Hugh smirked, snorting a little chuckle. "Isolda's mother was head cook when I was a boy; I was young myself when she was born. Better a faithful servant who'll speak her mind than an unfaithful one who won't speak at all."

"Hear, hear," Oswolf agreed.

"But why did you agree to Elfhar's request? And why did you

need *me* to come along?" Elena couldn't help but huff when she asked it, not caring if her annoyance showed. In her opinion, she'd earned the right to a little annoyance.

"Because I have a use for him," Hugh answered, keeping his eyes forward, scanning the road ahead of them. The land between Corfe and Wareham was a gently rolling series of flattened hillocks with swaying grasses and no trees to speak of. "If I play my pieces properly, Elfhar might be the solution we need to make sure that Corfe has the protection it requires."

"Truly? How do you propose to do that, Husband?"

"Easy, Wife." Hugh looked at her, tapping his temple with a sly smile. "I give him something he wants, and in return, he'll give me what I need."

"Namely defending the town, should it come under attack."

He nodded. "Precisely."

Elena huffed again, unable to help herself. "Less riddles, Husband, if you please. I'm uncomfortable enough at *one* end of me without you making my head hurt, as well."

Hugh's sly smile turned into a grin, but he kept more colorful commentary to himself. "Given what Ivan told us, Elfhar's wracked with guilt about what happened to Edward, and this plan of his that we're involved with is meant to assuage his guilty conscience. If I'm to assist him in that plan, I can broker favor with one of the most powerful ealdormen in the country, someone with resources on par with our young King himself. Since it's unlikely Æthelred—and, more appropriately, his mother—will lend us any aid, Elfhar will remember that favor and may repay it in kind if I request aid in some desperate hour of need."

Her mouth twisted up. "You'll pardon me, Husband, but it seems foolhardy to hang our hopes on a 'may', as it were."

"Don't think that hasn't occurred to me, starling." Hugh turned back to the road again. "But if it's what we have, if it can save our people, then 'may' is what I shall have to hang my hopes on, all the same."

"And what of me?" she said, softening her tone. "You insisted I should come as well, Lord. Why?"

The men looked at one another, then at her. "Didnae seem right that ye should b'excluded, lass," Oswolf answered. "Yer the only reason ol' Ed got a burial't all."

Hugh nodded.

Unsure of what to say to that, Elena was quiet for a long time. She harbored so many unwanted feelings and dark, angry thoughts towards the memories she had of the young king, cut down in his prime—Elena had watched it happen with her own eyes. Yet in spite of the crimes he'd performed upon her person, in spite of the fact she had every reason to hate him, Elena had indeed asked Elfrida for permission to bury Edward's body, once her men had finished their murderous work. In all of the time since, she'd never fully understood herself just why she'd spoken up at all. She still didn't, even then—maybe because it was the right thing to do; maybe because the idea of leaving his body to rot seemed even worse by comparison.

"Well, so long as I don't have to dig him up myself when we get there," she said with a frown. "I suppose I shall... persevere as best I can."

Then they rode on in silence, accompanied only by the sound of the horses' hooves on the hard road and the warm, spring breeze whistling in their ears. Elena puzzled over her thoughts and that one, lingering question, but the answer refused to show itself.

A SAD REUNION

*T*he parish church where young King Edward was buried was a long, rectangular, unfriendly-looking building of weathered grey stone. The graveyard accompanying it was vast, a wide swath of deep green dotted with dark markers, some so old and covered with moss and lichen that they were impossible to read. Elena remembered the unnaturally chilly day when they brought Edward's body, wrapped in a bloodstained sheet, to lay him to rest in secret—no one saw them arrive, and due to the heavy rain, no one came out to find them or saw them leave.

That day, the sun was shining and Elena didn't even need a shawl or cloak to warm herself. A young, very nervous looking cleric in formal ecclesial garb was standing next to an older man in a long, multicolored robe and a white mitre on his head, with a long, polished bronze staff topped with a small cross in his slender hands. The cleric was unknown to Elena, but she recognized Dunstan, Archbishop of Canterbury, immediately. He looked almost exactly the same as the day she'd met him, several years earlier. If anything, the years had made him slightly thinner, longer in the face, more severe and pinched-looking—it was not the sort of face a woman could easily forget.

Standing near Dunstan was another man Elena didn't know, but given that Ivan Black-Neck was next to him, she presumed him to be Ealdorman Elfhar. He was short with a bit of a paunch, greying hair shorn close to his scalp. He had no visible proof of any sort of office, but any sort of man that had earned the service of a man like Ivan Black-Neck had authority. Several armed men stood nearby, wearing colors Elena didn't recognize, but they flanked Ivan and the ealdorman. A short distance away, a number of laborers stood to one side, carrying pick-axes and shovels, talking to one another as they waited to be called upon.

Hugh confirmed it, speaking low as they approached, still on horseback, "That's Elfhar. Mind yourself if you speak to either of them, starling. No man amasses the sort of power either Elfhar or Dunstan has without good reason." He stepped out of the saddle, and Oswolf followed suit. Elena stayed in her seat, handing over the reins to her husband, who led both horses behind him as they approached.

Elena didn't feel the need to point out that Elfhar and Dunstan were obviously in some kind of league together—the fact that both the Archbishop and rival Ealdorman were ready and waiting for their arrival meant that some kind of arrangement had likely been made before Ivan ever showed up on Hugh's doorstep. If she had noticed it, she was sure Hugh had, as well.

The ealdorman spoke first as the trio approached, raising his arms in greeting. "Hugh! So good of you to accept my invitation."

"Elfhar," Hugh said as the other man approached. The two men embraced one another before Hugh turned to make introductions. "My wife, Elena—she's heavy with child, but I asked her to accompany us today. Also, our parish priest, Oswolf of Berwick."

Oswolf bowed his head. "Milord." Elena did the same.

"Ah, welcome." Elfhar reached up, taking Elena's hand; his fingers were thick, stubby, but his touch felt strangely hot somehow. "My apologies for the unhappy occasion, my dear."

"It's nothing, Lord," Elena said, shaking her head.

The short Ealdorman turned and gestured to Dunstan, who watched the goings-on with quiet, unfriendly eyes. "Your Grace, have you been introduced to Lord Isarnon and his companions?"

"We've met," Dunstan said. His voice was cool, yet still reminded Elena of the aural equivalent of sand grinding against bare flesh. The Archbishop struck Elena as an altogether unhappy person; she couldn't even try to imagine him smiling. The nameless church rector, the younger cleric who ran the church, followed behind Dunstan but didn't speak.

Oswolf went to one knee, took Dunstan's offered right hand, and kissed the ring he wore on it. "Yer Grace," he said.

"My son," Dunstan said in a perfunctory manner. "To your feet, and let's get on with it." The Archbishop eyed Elena for a moment, lingering on her belly, then apparently dismissed her from his mind altogether as he looked to Hugh. "Where is the body, Lord Isarnon?"

"Close," Hugh answered. He looked up to Elena. "Do you remember where the plot you picked was?"

Every eye in the group swiveled to her, and Elena had to fight an instinctive urge to clam up—she wasn't used to being the center of attention, and didn't particularly enjoy the sensation. Instead, she rose up a little higher in the saddle, using the vantage point she had to scan the burial ground, searching her memory for any familiar markers. When she spotted one, Elena nodded, pointing away from the church. "It was on the periphery of the yard, Lord. A corner spot, if memory serves."

Her husband nodded, taking the reins of both horses again, and led the way in the direction she'd indicated. Elfhar and Dunstan followed, with Oswolf right behind. Ivan Black-Neck gave a sharp whistle and a motion, and the other men, soldiers and laborers both, followed as well.

The burial place of Edward, son of Edgar, was as plain and unadorned as likely any king had ever received—the marker Elena had placed at its head was just a rough, rounded stone with a flat bottom. In the years since she'd placed it, moss had crept over it, and the grass was so thick it seemed unlikely that anyone thought anyone was buried there at all. "This is the place, my Lord," she said.

Hugh grunted, handing the reins of his horse to her. Then he turned to Elfhar, motioning to the spot. "This is it."

"Very good," the fat ealdorman said. "Ivan, get the men working here. Make sure they take care to disturb the body as little as possible."

"Yes, Lord," Ivan answered. Then, with a soldier's bluster and professional manner, he put the laborers to work, and soon the only sounds were of tools tearing away at the earth, and of hard breathing as the work was done. They made good time, piling the earth to one side, while laying out a long white cloth in the other in preparation for the bones that were to be found, blessed, wrapped up and carried away for safekeeping.

Elfhar and Dunstan watched the work with some detached interest, talking to one another quietly. Hugh simply watched, saying nothing. Nobody paid any attention to Elena, who elected to stay on her horse—however uncomfortable a seat it might've been, it seemed a better choice than having to stand around, being ignored.

And then, to her surprise, Ivan Black-Neck walked over, smiling a hello. "You English are a curious folk," he said. He had a pair of long pieces of grass in his fingers, which he set to his lips and gently blew out a breath, creating a sort of musical note.

"I suppose that all people are curious to someone," she said. "Are we so strange to you?"

"My people long most for an honorable death—in battle,

preferably, lest we grow too fat or lazy, or let our guard down." He looked up at the sky, and Elena could see the black band of his tattoo stretched all the way around his neck, likely explaining the epithet attached to his name, though not how it got there. "The way to Valhalla is reached only through fire; the gods require we burn our dead—those left behind in the cold earth are lost forever." Again, he blew a note through the grass pieces. "Did your dead king die honorably, Lady Iron Hand?"

Elena slowly shook her head. "He was murdered, actually," she said in a soft, sad voice. "No one deserves that sort of death."

"And you helped bury him?" Ivan sounded impressed.

"My husband did—he and the priest," she said, motioning to Oswolf, standing close-by. "I merely suggested it. Wanting to give the dead an honorable burial is... our way, I suppose."

Ivan nodded in understanding. The beads and bits of bone in his yellow beard clicked together. "Then it was good that you did this thing for him. Will his death be avenged, do you think?"

"I don't know. Perhaps, if God is just, his murderers would be punished, but... the world can be a cruel place." She looked at the Dane, pursing her lips thoughtfully. "If I might ask..."

He nodded. "Go ahead."

"How did you get the..." Her voice faded as she drew an invisible line around her neck.

"Oh, this?" He pulled his beard back with a smirk, baring the tattoo for her to see. "My father, Guthfrid, was a *jarl*—a great leader of men from across the sea. When he died, I became jarl. I led my men here, to fight your men and take their women— many of my people do such things, I mean no offense."

Elena thought it best to keep silent, so she did.

He continued, "But my men, they believed they could find a better leader than I, so they said they will no longer follow me. They sold me to slavers, and I came to this land not as a conqueror, but as a slave." He shrugged, appearing to take that development in stride, which she supposed was admirable enough. "Eventually, Elfhar of Mercia became my Master. He heard my story, found a use for me, granted me my freedom. Now I serve him. I am not a jarl, but that is beyond my control now. If I ever find the men who betrayed me, I will cut them down, or fall in battle with honor. And this," he gently tapped the side of his neck with a pair of fingers, "reminds me of what it meant to serve men, rather than to lead them. If the time ever comes to choose, I will cut off my own head rather than wear a collar ever again."

It was a short, unpleasant story, or so Elena thought. Oswolf cleared his throat. "'Tis a sad tale, though'm glad ye made't through t'the other side, good Ivan."

"And I, as well," Ivan agreed. "If the world were just, all murderers, slavers and betrayers would meet the same fate they dole out to others."

"Agreed," said the Scot.

Elena looked up. The sun was shining from behind a thick head of white clouds. The wind was slow, pleasant and enough to keep her brow cool. She rested her hand over her stomach, stroking it slowly, almost tenderly. Ivan blew another soft, musical note with his grass-whistle.

Elfhar motioned to Ivan, who dropped the grass pieces and brushed his hands on his leather breeks. "Excuse me," he said, walking over to his Lord again.

"S'all comin' full circle, ain't't," Oswolf said in a soft voice as the Dane departed, standing next to Elena's horse. All three of the beasts had their heads down, eating some of the thick tufts of grass at their feet.

"How do you mean, Father?"

"Think about't, lass—the lad goes t'Hugh's Hall, winds up dead; we bring'm 'ere, lay the poor soul to rest; now we're back 'ere, diggin' 'im up again, in the hopes'f it helpin' protect the very place where Edward died t'begin with. I daresay Ol' Ed deserves a proper place to rest 'is 'ead fer a spell."

"Yes." Elena watched the laborers work, talking amongst themselves or focusing on their hard, sweaty work. "It wasn't right—what happened to Edward, I mean. I don't know how just the world can be when men like Ivan Black-Neck come to raid our villages, or murderous Queen Regents go unpunished. Edward trusted Elfrida... and look where he ended up for it." She kept her voice carefully low, not wanting to risk the others overhearing her—the matter of Elfrida's involvement in her stepson's death was still a sensitive subject, at least as far as Elena was concerned. For most people, it probably appeared the young king had gone off riding by himself and disappeared, never to be seen by the inhabitants of Winchester or the royal court ever again. Æthelred's coronation was conducted by default, since the country needed a ruler, but it was no surprise people were elevating Edward's memory into something more mythical or holier than he ever was when he was alive.

Oswolf nodded. The Scot was so tall they could look eye to eye while he stood flat-footed on the ground.

"Am I wrong for hating the man's memory, Father? Is that so very horrible of me?" Elena didn't have to explain to Oswolf why she harbored such feelings—he'd been there, both before and after the beating happened. He'd tried to save her from Edward's wrath, albeit unsuccessfully. He'd seen the wounds with his own eyes.

The priest sighed. "'Tis true, lass, what the Good Book says: 'Querellum sicut et Dominus donavit vobis'—that is, 'Fergive as t'Lord fergave ye,' ye ken. I dinnae think the Almighty would fail t'understand yer grievance wit' what Edward did t'ye... but, on t'other hand, I would t'ink, given what price he ultimately paid fer the ambitions'f others... perhaps y'*might* consider cuttin' the lad a bit'f slack." Oswolf spread his hands. "Or don't. 'Tis yer choice'n all."

Elena twisted up her mouth. Oswolf was a family friend, one

she cared for immensely, but sometimes his advice was positively unhelpful. It wasn't that she didn't appreciate it, but—

The sound of a scream broke through her thoughts. By now, the hole dug into Edward's grave was perhaps half as deep as Elena was tall. One of the laborers was down on his knees, brushing away something in the dirt, when he shrieked and jumped out of the hole, scrambling back on all fours like a wild thing. Underneath the streaks of dirt, the man's face was white as death, and he continually crossed himself, over and over, whimpering something under his breath while several of his companions tried to comfort him.

"What's happening?" Elena said.

"M'not sure," Oswolf said with a frown. "'Scuse me, Elena." Leaving his horse to graze on its own—indeed, none of the animals seemed to care about the man's terror in any way—the priest quickly stepped over to check on him, kneeling down and whispering something as he bent over the man. Elena watched as Hugh, Elfhar and Dunstan all approached the grave, peering into it as another one of the laborers motioned and spoke in low, clipped tones. Whatever the first man had uncovered, no one came anywhere near it.

Wanting to see, not wanting to see, Elena grimaced and took a firm hold of the saddle. Somehow she managed to get down to the ground without twisting her ankle or landing on her head, and after a moment to smooth her skirts, she walked past Oswolf and the other laborers, wading through the thick grass and up to her husband's side where he stood over the hole in the ground.

"Ah, Lady," Elfhar interjected when he saw her approaching, "perhaps you'd best keep back."

"Pardon, my Lord," she answered, managing to stay respectful, "but I'm the reason that young man was buried there at all. What has happened?"

Dunstan gave Hugh an unfriendly look. "Control your wife,

Lord Isarnon, or I shall see that she's controlled for you." The tone of his voice twisted in Elena like a bellyful of spoiled fruit.

"Yes, Your Grace," Hugh said. And yet, he didn't reach over to take hold of Elena's arm until she'd stepped next to him and had a chance to look down into Edward's grave. The memory of the man's panicked scream and the sight of his face left her uncertain, even afraid, but she had to see what caused it for herself.

Inside the hole, the dirt brushed back, Elena saw Edward's face and hands, clasped over his breast. The dead man was holding a cup to his chest, the same cup that Elfrida had offered to welcome him when the young king had arrived at Hugh's Hall at the Queen's own invitation, having ridden all the way from Winchester without an escort. Even as he raised that cup to quench his thirst, Elfrida's men had surrounded him, pulled Edward out of the saddle and stabbed him to death.

But now she could see what had frightened the laborer so, and her own heart nearly stilled when she noticed it: Edward was pale, very pale, as seemed befitting to a man long-dead, but otherwise his face and body appeared to be completely unspoiled. If his breast had moved, as though merely asleep, it wouldn't have surprised Elena to see it—he seemed so lifelike, with no touch of the grave or decay on him anywhere that she could see.

"A miracle!" the cleric cried, already on his knees next to the grave, crucifix clutched in his trembling hands. "Surely, God Himself has shown us a blessing this day!"

More of the workers took another step back, crossing themselves as well, not that Elena could blame them. It wasn't natural that a corpse should still be whole after such a long time in the ground. Elena didn't resist as Hugh led her away, back to the horses; the hand on her arm was loose, more for appearances than anything else.

"They're frightened," he said, under his breath.

"Can you blame them? *I'm* frightened," she said, remembering the dead man's face with a shudder. "How is it even possible?"

"I don't know, starling. For now, watch and wait." He gave her arm a comforting squeeze and withdrew back to the gravesite, where Elfhar and Dunstan were either talking or arguing in sharp, hushed tones. The man Oswolf was tending to had some of his color back, but he refused to approach the grave again, and left under the watchful eye of a companion as they headed back to town. The cleric continued his fervent prayers, but he spoke in Latin, which she couldn't follow.

Elena narrowed her eyes and tried to concentrate, to focus on what the Archbishop and Elfhar were arguing about. It was difficult to make it out, even at such a short distance, until Dunstan raised his voice, "—say that he shall be removed to Canterbury, Lord Elfhar, under my supervision. The body will need to be preserved, relics must be collected and cataloged for affirmation, everything must be carefully and meticulously handled according to Church law." Dunstan crossed himself, with a rare flush in his narrow cheeks. "A miraculous sign such as this one cannot be handled lightly."

"But, surely there must be another way, Your Grace!" Elfhar sounded pained. "Just transporting the body may take weeks, and after so much time and expense, it may be months before a proper burial befitting the good King can be performed. Surely you don't believe that a miracle such as this one can be trusted to last so long as that."

"Be that as it may," Dunstan answered in his cold, dry manner, "I have nowhere else that can be trusted to hold this body safely and securely for the time being."

Knowing it would rile him, not caring, Elena spoke up. "That's not entirely true, Your Grace."

The Archbishop scowled at her, looked over at Hugh. "Lord, I warned you—"

Elena kept talking. "The abbey at Shaftesbury should suit

your needs, Your Grace. It's much closer than Canterbury, and Shaftesbury falls under my husband's jurisdiction, so the body would be well-protected." Hugh's face was impossible to decipher, but if there were consequences to pay later, Elena would pay them gladly—whatever it took to tweak old Dunstan's nose. "And I believe King Edward's grandmother Elgiva died and was buried there. If my memory serves," she added.

Oswolf spoke up. "Aye, the Lady speaks true, Yer Grace. An' King Edward's gran'mother Wynflæd was abbess there s'well, I believe. S'the King would be among family... as't were," he added, his voice faltering a bit under the Archbishop's unfriendly stare.

Dunstan and Hugh looked at one another. Hugh finally dipped his head in acknowledgement. "She speaks truthfully, Your Grace. By your leave, I can have the body moved to the abbey by tonight."

To say the Archbishop looked displeased was an understatement, but he seemed to give it some honest thought, all the same. Finally, he nodded. "Very well, then. Elfhar, get your men to dig out the body, and make sure they do so *carefully*. Isarnon, take your busybody of a wife home, then I expect you to oversee the transportation of Edward to the abbey personally."

"Yes, Your Grace," the two ealdormen said, practically in unison.

Elena tried not to look smug. She very nearly managed it, in fact.

A PAINFUL HAND

"You were baiting him." Hugh sounded... well, *'perturbed'* was the word that came to Elena's mind.

"I was *not* baiting him, Husband," she answered. "I simply showed the Archbishop that my husband 'controlling' me doesn't mean I can't have better ideas than he does."

It was quite late, and the solitary candle clock on the nearby wall said it was well after midnight. The ride home from Wareham earlier that day was rather quiet but uneventful, save for a slow, lingering discomfort Elena had—it was deep in her belly, lower down, even more than where she was sure the baby's head rested. It was uncomfortable but bearable, so she waited until it went away and decided to mention it to Isolda on the next morning when the midwife would check in on her again.

Before he left, Hugh promised they'd "discuss things" when he returned later that evening. Seeing as that was a promise he intended to return home, Elena sat up and waited for him in bed, sipping at another cup of watered-down small ale to soothe her stomach. Isolda had shared all sorts of strange, quasi-mystical theories about how to predict the sex of her baby—everything from the thickness and hue of Elena's hair, whether one breast was larger than the other, even if she was ever exceptionally clumsy—but Elena stuck to the absolute certainty she was having a boy. Supposedly, even the color of her urine could be a predictor, but the only thing Elena had noticed going into the ninth month was she sometimes needed a trip to the chamber pot two or maybe even three times a night.

"Elena." The man stopped, one leg already out of his pants, and gave her a long, steady look.

While already undressed for bed—which is to say she wasn't dressed at all—Elena felt vulnerable, even uncomfortable, under that sort of stare. She squirmed in bed, looking down at the cup in her hands, and sighed. "Did I cause you undue grief, my Lord?"

"None I wasn't prepared to accept or couldn't handle on my own," he said; she heard the rustling of fabric as he continued undressing. "I believe I give you more than enough freedom to speak your mind in my house—as do most of the women in it," he added under his breath, "but antagonizing the Archbishop is a tad much."

"Well, he deserved it," Elena said, looking up again, setting her cup to one side. She crossed both arms, resting them across her stomach, letting out a breath somewhere between a huff and a sigh. "The man was an ass when I met him after Edgar died, and time hasn't done a *single* thing to improve that."

"A salient point," Hugh countered, sitting down on the edge of the bed, "and one not too far off the mark, in my estimate. But I *told* you to be mindful of what you said, Elena; we were in public, with witnesses, other men watching and listening—men *I* have to deal with, who observe *your* behavior and believe it reflects upon *me*. Was it really so much to ask you to remember *that*?" For a long moment, his eyes held Elena hostage—she was unable to move or hardly even to speak; the only reason she kept breathing was because her body willed it so. The only thing showing time hadn't stopped was the steady, solitary flicker of the candle's flame in the distance, showing half of his face in light, and the other gone black in shadow. He was displeased, she knew that much, and those consequences she'd flaunted earlier were coming back to her now.

It was humbling and humiliating, the way Elena felt, when she pushed away from the pillows, going onto her hands and knees again. The last time had been willing on her part, a ploy to tease and tempt him. Now she stretched out completely onto the bed, her knees bent for the sake of cradling her swollen tummy, but she stretched her arms above her head and turned her face away, staring into the dark shadows of their bedroom. She didn't want to look at Hugh, didn't want to face his anger or—worse— his disappointment.

Whether it was her husband's place to discipline her or not, Elena wouldn't look at him when he did so. Discipline for the sake of pleasure was one thing, but doing it for the sake of punishment reminded her too much of the cold, loveless years of their marriage. She closed her eyes, let out a long breath, and waited.

She didn't have to wait for very long, though. The feel of his bare hand striking her upraised backside was hard, somehow stinging worse than the leather belt he'd wielded the night before. Elena turned her head, trying to muffle her whimpering into the blanket, but he was relentless. He wanted to hear her cry out, she knew, but some of her old stubbornness flared back to life inside of her, trying to hold out, not wanting to give him what he wanted. She could be strong and could defy him for a little while... couldn't she? Why should he tell her when to speak or what to say?

In seconds, her bottom was burning from the assault, stinging like he was dragging nettles across her flesh. Elena opened her mouth and bit down on the blanket, squeezing any unshed tears out of her eyes as she pressed her face down in the empty hope her cries could be hushed or stifled somehow, yet

Hugh gave her no relief, no chance to escape even one of those hard strikes which seemed to always catch some part of her bottom that hadn't yet felt the harsh bite of his discipline. Eventually she turned on the bed, rolling her bottom away from him, trying to curl up into as tight of a ball as her belly allowed; she cried, and let him hear her cries, the painful sobbing made worse by how she wanted more—more punishment, more discipline, more pain and pleasure. At that moment she hated she wanted more, hated that the heat in her abdomen meant she'd enjoyed his spanking.

"Mercy," she cried, gasping it aloud in-between her panicked, hungry breathing. "No more, Hugh, please... Please, no more."

"My poor, starling," he said, his voice the low hum of a whisper. He didn't continue the spanking, but rather rolled her onto her back on the bed; the rough blankets itched against her tender bottom and Elena whimpered again, pushing up on the balls of her feet to relieve the discomfort.

That was just what Hugh had been waiting for. The way the fingers of both hands grabbed onto her ass, squeezing it tight, lifting her even higher off the bed, made her gasp and cry out again, so she pressed her hand against her mouth and bit down to quiet herself. Fresh tears leaked out the corner of her eyes as she watched him, a hulking shadow in the dark, hanging over her like a vengeful spirit of lust and righteous anger. The feeling of his manhood, hard and ready, pressed against her lower lips made Elena want more and want to push away at the same moment. She felt some irrational urge to be free of him, while also wanting to roll back onto her knees and thrust her moist, swollen quim back at him like an animal in heat.

Penetration was quick, a long thrust of his flesh that filled her to the brim in one push—now her hushed cry turned into a moan instead. She pulled her own hand away from her mouth, seeing no reason to quiet herself any longer, and held tight to the blankets in both hands as he took her. It was a strange, surreal experience to be half-floating off the bed, held aloft by his hands and muscled arms, filled to bursting with his flesh. He controlled the pace, which was blissfully quick, a wet slapping of flesh to flesh; liquid sounds of raw sex filled Elena's ears and she began to feel like she was completely weightless, ready to float away if not for the way he held her down. Her body was under his control, burning with fevered want, gone cold with the need for release. Every second she didn't orgasm was a second she was sure her heart would burst in her chest.

"H-help," she said, a choked whimper. "Help m-me, Hugh. Please." Her fingernails dug into his arms, leaving shallow furrows in his flesh. "Please!"

"What is it?" he said, immediately slowing down, but not stopping.

Elena couldn't speak, could barely do more than form the single thought that was screaming in her head. She reached around her belly, stretching, trying to find her clit—one touch would do it, she was sure of it. If she didn't find some kind of relief, she was going to die. He had to understand, surely, he had to!

Somehow, whether by a miracle or otherwise, he did. What she couldn't reach, he could. Elena's legs trembled as she was set back onto the trembling balls of her feet, allowing him to continue his driving rhythm, and now he had one hand free. Licking the tip of his thumb, he reached down between them, swirling the tip of it around her tiny bud, a familiar motion he'd used dozens, hundreds, even thousands of times. She couldn't see his touch, but Elena could feel it like a crack of thunder shaking her to her very core.

Heat built up, arching up her back, shooting down between her thighs and back up again in her head where it exploded. She came so hard she saw stars, colors in the periphery of her vision she'd never seen before. Her body went rigid as Hugh went back to fucking her with such vigor and energy he seemed possessed by it. Elena floated on a cloud of warmth and pleasure until he came a minute later, and gently laid her back down on the bed again. She no longer cared about or even felt any sort of discomfort. The thick, pungent seed he'd spilled in her was a stain between her opened legs, bits of it still oozing out of him as he sat on his hindquarters, panting for breath, as though he even lacked the energy to lie down.

On occasion, intimacy with her husband was hot and messy. Good sex was like that, sometimes.

Once Elena had the energy to sit up, her body ached just a little bit more, and her bottom was certainly throbbing from his attention, which wasn't necessarily a bad thing. She wanted to go to him, but something held her back—reluctance, fear, maybe some lingering humiliation from earlier. Their eyes met, and she fought the urge to start trembling. It wasn't that she wanted to hesitate, but the memory of his displeasure was still fresh, and she hated the idea of exacerbating it even further.

When Hugh opened his arms, Elena flung herself to him, her heart suddenly pounding, her blood gone cold. The feel of his skin against hers was comforting, and she wrapped her arms around him, face pressed to his breast. She kissed him, over and over, compelled to do it by a force she couldn't name, but one which felt so overwhelming she felt new tears at the corners of her eyes. "I'm sorry," she whispered, several times over. "I'm sorry, I'm sorry. Please forgive me."

"Sh," he said, his warm, strong hands on her shoulders, her back, cupped under the curve of her bottom. "I'm not sure how much there is for me to even forgive, starling—you did nothing that I didn't expect of you."

God, but he felt good: warm, solid, so large and wonderful to the touch. Her stomach, as well as the lingering soreness of the day and the fresh ache in her reddened backside, made it harder for her to turn in his arms. Eventually she managed to stretch her legs out on the bed, resting her head on his shoulder, one hand on his chest while the other clung tight to his waist. "Then I'm *not* sorry," she said with a slight huff. "Not to him, anyway. I hate that I might have caused you any sort of disrespect—I never meant anything of the kind, my love. Truly."

"I know, Elena, I know." The feel of his kiss atop her head, the same kind he'd given her countless times before, made her heart beat faster. "But this won't be the last we see of the good Archbishop—promise me you'll tuck that sharp tongue of yours away when it comes to him."

Elena looked up the line of one bare, bent leg, across his stomach and ribs, the broad chest with its thick curtain of dark hair, like some kind of wild thing. His face was still the kind, loving visage she'd fallen in love with over the past year, but his eyes were steady, boring into her, pinning her down in place. She could sooner break a steel blade than break that gaze, and it both aroused and frightened her again to look at it.

The power Hugh Isarnon had over her was wonderful, and it was terrifying at the same time. The man was as naked as she, and he wouldn't have looked more formidable if he'd been dressed for battle.

"I promise," she whispered.

He looked at her for a moment, then nodded. "Good. Then that's enough."

Neither of them seemed to want to move, not even to settle in amongst the pillows again. Elena felt good in Hugh's arms, and even though she knew they couldn't linger there forever, for the time being she closed her eyes and sighed happily, basking in the closeness of him like a cat soaking in the sunshine. The pleasure was so small, so simple and understated, yet she wouldn't exchange it for the world. But then the discomfort in her womb from earlier that day returned—her brow furrowed and she closed her eyes, blowing out a long, deep breath of frustration.

"Elena?"

"M-my apologies," she said, shaking her head. "It's just... a distraction, Husband. Something I felt earlier on the ride back today—I expect I must've hurt myself in the saddle somehow." The painful pressure was down, deep down again, somehow stronger than the sharp pangs she'd felt on Sybil's arm the previous day, and yet not as strong—it didn't hurt as much, but it lasted longer. Hugging her lover tighter in her arms, she pressed her cheek hard to his chest, and waited for it to pass, wishing it would go away.

Except it didn't. The pain lessened after a few moments, and she took a cleansing breath as she sat up straighter in bed, one hand pressed low on the underside of her belly, but it didn't vanish completely. Now it was merely uncomfortable again, a slow, grinding sensation that reminded her of her menses.

"Are you sure you're all right?" he said.

"I-I'm not sure," Elena said, looking up at him. When the pain didn't stop, she licked her lips; when it increased again, growing with the same intensity and dull fire as before, she closed her eyes and clenched her teeth. God, no, why did it have to be *now*?

Something was different this time—she was sure of it.

Elena opened her eyes. "I think you may need to fetch Sybil and Isolda for me now."

A NEW ARRIVAL

*I*n minutes, both maidservant and midwife were present in the room and had taken control of the situation: Hugh was bid a firm, unquestionable farewell, with the promise of news whenever there was any to share, and Sybil got several younger members of the cooking staff out of bed and to work fetching towels and boiling water. She also refreshed the candle clock and lit candles around the room until the glow was at a level that Elena could withstand.

The Lady stood by the side of her bed, still stripped to her skin, while Isolda was behind her, applying massaging pressure to Elena's scarred back.

"You should think about putting your gown back on, Milady," Sybil said as she busied herself slowly pulling the oak chests away from the bed. She was pulling all of the furniture to the far side of the room, making as much space around the bed as possible.

"Why?" Elena gave a breathy laugh as the latest series of contractions began slowing down, the pain once again fading away in lieu of that uncomfortable-but-bearable grinding pressure between her legs. "Taking my clothes off is what got me into this mess in the first place, remember?"

The taller brunette opened her mouth to answer, then closed it as she went back to dragging furniture.

"See how it feels, Milady," Isolda urged in a gentle voice. She reached over, picked up the gown draped over the edge of the bed, and began to pull it over Elena's head.

"Stop, stop," Elena said, raising a hand to push the gown away. The fabric barely even touched her, yet she was sure it was going to strangle her. She didn't care about embarrassment, about what anybody could see—she wanted to be as free as possible, whether that meant unabashed nakedness or not. Another wave of hot, heavy pain filled her up, rolled over her belly and bore down between her legs. She shook her head, but couldn't speak, leaning over the bed.

Isolda tossed the gown away. "If you're a squeamish sort, Sybil, I'm sure the girls in the kitchen could use an extra pair of hands." The older woman's tone was curt, even dismissive.

"N-no." Elena raised her head, even though the contractions were still ongoing. "Sybil can stay." She opened her eyes, looking at her maidservant. She could see it plain in the other woman's eyes, Sybil was worried, even afraid.

But then, so was Elena. Her pregnancy had gone remarkably well, all things considered, but birthing the child in her belly was a terrifying prospect. It was anyone's guess as to whether her labor would be difficult or not—her chances were good, but plenty of healthy women didn't survive to see the child they delivered, assuming the child survived at all. Elena was an only child, a side effect of just how traumatic her own birth had been on Helen, her mother. Would the same thing happen to her?

The dark-haired maidservant hesitated for half of a moment, then nodded. "Very well. I'll stay and I won't get in anyone's way," she added, throwing Isolda a firm look.

The midwife nodded. "See that you don't. For now, come here."

"W-what? Why?"

"Because I told you to." Isolda's tone had little in the way of patience, and Sybil practically jumped like a startled cat before hurrying over. "Now, put your hands here—" Elena felt one above her left hip, another at the base of her spine. "—and here. Keep them there, gently rub the muscle. When she pushes at you, push back hard, just don't tip her over like a teakettle." Isolda bent in close to Elena's ear. "Milady, I'll be back soon."

Elena nodded sharply, not speaking, waiting for the contraction to subside. Her heart was pounding in her chest, flush with adrenaline and fear, but at least the pain didn't somehow get worse. With her eyes closed, she heard Isolda's soft steps move to the door, heard it open and shut a second later. The pain finally began to fade again a moment later, and she pushed back towards Sybil, enjoying the pressure of the woman's hands that drowned out the strain between her legs. "Mmm, thank you," she said, her voice sounding like a drunken hum.

"Of course," Sybil said, sounding a little uncomfortable, but doing as she was bid without complaint. "My apologies, Milady."

"Why?"

"Well..." The maidservant sounded flustered. "I didn't mean for my embarrassment to... to be a distraction."

"Here." Elena reached around, moving one of Sybil's hands to her other hip, then pushed back again. Such a simple thing, yet somehow it felt amazing. "You don't have to apologize," Elena answered, looking over her shoulder with a worn smile. Nobody had told her labor would be so tiring—and the night was just beginning. "I'm glad you stayed, though."

"Milady?"

"You're my friend, Sybil. I didn't want to be alone during all of... this." She waved a hand in a helpless sort of gesture before going down to both hands again. The contractions would be picking up again in another moment.

"Am I, truly?" Sybil sounded surprised.

Elena nodded. "I've always thought so. I remember how we were both so awkward around each other when you first came here, all those years ago."

Sybil flushed, but still smiled. "*I* remember the time I thought you were calling me in the middle of the night, except I walked in on you and Lord Hugh... well..." Now Sybil's flush turned into a full-on blush.

It made Elena laugh, in spite of the pain. She couldn't help it, and winced afterward, even as her shoulders kept shaking. "And you couldn't... look me in the eye... the whole next day! You just kept apologizing... over and over."

"Well, what *else* was I supposed to do?" Sybil said in protest, her massaging fingers digging in deep enough to make Elena wince; after that, she eased up a bit. "Is it... is it very painful?" she said next, her brow furrowing in concern. "I always worry I won't be able to handle it if my time ever comes."

"It's... unpleasant, certainly," Elena said, "but, it's nothing compared to what will come from it." She smiled, resting a hand down on her stomach, as if she could feel the little one stirring and moving inside. "Shouldn't you be looking for a man yourself by now, Sybil? You can't stay a maiden forever. People will talk."

"Is this really the right time to discuss this?" Sybil said, sounding alarmed.

Apparently it wasn't. Another contraction hit and Elena lost her voice, her breath, everything but the pain—her whole body hurt, tightening up, spreading down her body and belly again. She gritted her teeth, clenched her hands tight in the blankets in front of her and waited for the endless, agonizing moment to end. It held, and held, and lasted and kept going and refused to end... until it was finally over.

Elena picked her head up again. "Have you... got anything...

better to do right now?" she said with a huff when she caught her breath. "It's a distraction and I could use more of those right now. It's better than making myself worry that something's going to go wrong somehow."

"Well…"

"What about Hefner, the brewer? Or someone down in Corfe?" Elena leaned on her elbows, rocking slowly back and forth for the pleasure of it, letting her head hang down. A sudden thought occurred to her. "What about Oswolf?"

Sybil jerked so much she nearly pushed Elena over. "The *priest*? You thought of *him*, Milady?"

The way she said it made Elena laugh again. "And why not? I remember the trip the four of us took to Winchester two years ago, after King Edgar died—you two looked good together."

"I, ah… I'm not sure," Sybil said, sounding hesitant, "i-if this is the best time to be discussing that sort of thing, you understand."

It was easier to breathe when the contractions slowed, so Elena had enough energy to look back and smile at Sybil. "You've been a good and faithful servant, one I've been proud to have with me all this time. I just want you to have a chance at happiness the same way I finally found mine. Everyone deserves a chance to be happy."

"You're very kind, Milady," Sybil said with a small, relieved looking smile. "But don't think about me for now. I'm worried for you, mostly. If I can do anything…"

"It's fine," Elena said, cutting her off as more pain came. "Just… stay with me."

After that, Elena went quiet and let her body take control— breathing soft, shallow breaths during the painful times, breathing deeper and slower as the pain ebbed. Isolda and Sybil traded off responsibilities as was necessary, letting their Lady's senses float about on a grey cloud of consciousness. Her entire world became an unending wave of painful contractions, lasting for long, breathless moments, and then easing down to something bearable for just a little while. Elena did what she could to mitigate the pain—slowly walking in circles around the room, leaning over the bed and gyrating her hips, rocking to and fro on her hands and knees, even resting her head on the soft shoulder of one woman while the other hurried off on this errand or that one. Towels were soaked in the steaming-hot water, wrung out, and then laid across her back while she rested beside the bed, rocking back and forth in time with the contractions. She moaned with the pain, shivered when it ended. It was unlike anything she'd ever felt before, and it seemed like it might never end. She was exhausted after a time, lacking even the energy to look at or ask what time it was.

Elena was on her hands and knees on the rug beside the bed when the sudden shift happened. She felt a wet rush between her legs—she sniffed, smelling salt water, reminding her of years ago when she, Hugh, Oswolf and Sybil all rode aboard a sea vessel on the way to King Edgar's funeral. "What..." God, it was almost too much just to speak anymore. She opened her eyes, saw Isolda kneeling in front of her, looking as intent as ever. "What happened?" She heard footsteps, saw the swishing of skirts as the pair of kitchen girls withdrew from the room, carrying off the old towels and leaving behind fresh ones.

"Your water's broken, Milady," Isolda said with another rare smile. "You'll feel the urge to push soon—just let it happen. Your body will know what to do."

Sybil was mopping up the remnants of Elena's breakage, but after that the two women switched positions, with Sybil at the head and Isolda below. Isolda didn't tell Elena to move or climb onto the bed, which was good, because Elena didn't have the energy to do any such thing. More hot towels were draped across her back, but their blissful heat was minuscule compared to the intensity of the contractions by that point. No, they were something else. A raw, physical *urge* to tighten every muscle and bear down, pushing towards her bottom, all the way down into her toes. Elena began to moan again, growing in intensity, much louder now—not a scream, but a deep, guttural sound ringing in her throat that ended in a deep, cleaning howl that reverberated in her ears. It ended when the contraction ended, going back to that dull, grinding ache in her belly.

"Tired," Elena said, or whispered, or hissed, or whined—she couldn't even tell anymore. She fell forward onto Sybil, her head resting in the crook of the woman's neck.

"You'll feel it again in a second, Milady," Isolda said.

Elena didn't want to feel it again. She wanted to sleep.

Towels were removed, towels were replaced.

Heat. Comfort. Relief.

Then more of the same: more pain, more urging, more pushing. Elena's moan was as lewd and wicked as anything she'd ever made at the end of Hugh's cock—he could have only dreamt of coaxing such a noise from her as that one. God, she wished he was here right then, wished his cock was in her mouth. She'd have made *him* moan like that. That'd serve him right.

The urge to push subsided. More towels, more relief.

Isolda was saying something, and then the pain was back—sharper, clearer, like the edge of a blade splitting her in two. For a third time, she howled like a banshee as she pushed down, trying to empty herself out, to void the burning fullness between her legs. That effort earned her a moment's pause, a chance to catch her breath as she *felt* something—he was nearly out, she was sure of it.

One more push, one more bearing down, one more calling out for anyone to hear her: not a scream, but a wild, triumphant cry.

"He's out!" Isolda sounded overjoyed.

A second later, Elena heard the high-pitched, gurgling sound of a newborn's voice. She looked up, noticed that Sybil was crying, hugging her shoulders, smiling from ear to ear.

"Easy now, easy—hop to it, girl! Help her back." Isolda gave her orders with the air of a general going to war, and Sybil sniffed aloud but hurried to obey.

Elena was helped down onto her bottom on a makeshift bed of dry, soft towels and propped pillows. Elena noted, in some detached part of her brain, that there was surprisingly—thankfully—very little blood, save for a bit of a smear between her legs. Carefully, she was settled backwards, but already reaching for the tiny, messy little lump in Isolda's arms. The midwife handed it over, resting the babe on the new mother's bare chest.

He was larger than she'd expected, smeared head to toe in some waxy sort of substance, save for where his face was wiped clean. He had a thick mat of midnight-black hair, some of it sticking up from his little head practically on-end, and his dark eyes were open, to go with his mouth, which was already rooting at her chest as he whined in protest.

"Sh," Isolda said, silencing Elena's questions before she could say them aloud. The midwife helped her to guide his mouth to one of her nipples, where he latched on with a fervor that made her gasp with surprise. Isolda chuckled. "At least he won't need a lesson in *that*—though, they rarely do."

Elena was staring at his face, down at his eyes, cradling him in one arm while gently toying with his thick hair with her other hand.

"He's gorgeous," Sybil said in a whisper.

"And seems healthy to boot," Isolda said. "Milady."

Elena almost didn't hear it. Almost.

Isolda insisted. "Milady?"

Reluctantly, Elena looked up. She was astoundingly tired, yet suddenly felt like she didn't want to sleep at all if it meant she could keep watching the little one at her breast.

"You'll feel more pains in a moment—just let them come. The afterbirth will have to pass, then the cord snipped afterwards. There'll be some bleeding, so don't be alarmed."

"Oh. Y-yes, of course." It felt surreal, that the job somehow wasn't done yet. But Isolda knew her stuff, and as the newborn kept sucking, more contractions began again—only slightly less intense than before, but Elena moaned and trembled under their power all the same. Three times, they came and went, and Elena withstood them as best she could, until she gave a violent shudder as *something* released its hold on her and let go.

"There we go," Isolda said, catching something in a towel in her hands. She bent over it, checking for something Elena couldn't begin to guess at, and nodded with satisfaction before looking up again. "Well done, Milady. The deed is done."

Sybil was helping to pack fresh towels between Elena's legs to mop up any unpleasantness that came after, but Elena didn't trouble herself with that. She went back to looking at the newborn, touching his face with the gentlest caress she could muster. "Thank you," she said. There were tears in her eyes, she knew, and she didn't wipe them away as she looked up at the pair who'd carried her through the whole ordeal. "Truly. I don't know what I would have done..." She looked down at her baby again. "If you both hadn't been here."

"It was a pleasure," Sybil said, sniffing again.

"Ah, you needn't fret, Lady," Isolda said, as she went about the task of severing the cord and tying it off, working with quick, knowing fingers. "A woman knows her own body best. I'm sure you'd have figured it out, one way or another. And just wait until your next little one comes. Why, now you're practically a professional!"

Elena would have laughed if she'd had the energy. She did smile, at least. "Given how long it took and how I barely managed this one, I'm not sure how likely it is there'll be any others."

"We shall see, Milady," Isolda said in a sagacious manner. "We shall see."

After a short time, Sybil prepared the bed for Elena and later cleaned up the mess with little muss or fuss at all. Once she was in bed, the softness of it was a relief to Elena's sore posterior, and she sank down into it with a sigh and a little moan of satisfaction. "Oh, that *is* better," she said. By that time, she'd swapped her son from one breast to the other, and he continued to suckle as if he hadn't a moment to lose, now covered in a blanket while still pressed to her chest—Isolda insisted on that, saying something about its importance that Elena was too distracted to fully pay attention to.

"We'll bring his Lordship back in soon," Isolda said, "if you're ready to see him."

"Oh yes," Elena said with a nod. "Yes, of course."

"Has he chosen a name yet?" Sybil asked, collecting the spent towels into a basket for carrying. The furniture would be moved back into place another day.

"John," Elena said, looking at the little boy with yet another smile; her face was already hurting from smiling so much. "It was my father's name, and the Lord's great-grandfather's, as well."

"A good name," Isolda said, while Sybil nodded in agreement.

The women left, and for a few moments Elena was alone, or as close to alone as she might ever be for a while to come. She touched the boy's face, looked into his eyes, which by now were half-lidded already, likely as not, she expected he was tired too.

"My John," she whispered.

John, of course, was too preoccupied for much in the way of conversation, and had his mouth full besides.

Elena didn't even hear the door open or close again, but noticed a familiar weight settle down next to her in bed, a familiar arm slide around her bare shoulders. Hugh's breath was warm and wonderful in her hair. For a moment she closed her eyes and simply existed, content as she could be, or might be, ever again.

"The sun'll be up in less than an hour," he said. "Isolda said you were quite fast when it comes to this sort of thing."

She gave a sniff of a chuckle. "I might have fainted from exhaustion if it took any longer." Elena turned her head, nuzzling her nose into his beard, kissing his neck. "May I present you with your son, Milord Iron Hand—as your wife predicted months ago, I might add."

Hugh brushed his fingertips through the tuft of black hair, still standing straight up from the tiny, round head at her breast. "Truly a marvel," he said with wonder in his voice.

"And I've some shocking news to report, my Husband."

"What's that?"

Elena grinned at him. "In spite of my suspicions to the contrary, given who his father is, he doesn't *as yet* appear to have a beard."

A SURPRISING DEVELOPMENT

*N*o one was ever able to explain why Edward's body had failed to decay after his death. After the body was transported to Shaftesbury under armed guard with Hugh's direct supervision, it was placed in a coffin for temporary safe-keeping. Relics were collected under Dunstan's watchful eye to send to Rome to confirm they were truly touched by Divinity. Hugh was content to leave him alone to do whatever pleased him, and Elena was in accord with that plan—now that their son was born, she loathed the thought of her husband leaving again, especially to babysit someone as persnickety as the Archbishop. Isolda insisted on Elena spending a full day in bed, due to prolonged bleeding and waiting for her milk to come in, but she was itching to get up and was out of bed in less than half of that. Aside from the discomfort and aching in her breasts as her body transitioned from pregnancy to new motherhood—not to mention how eager John was whenever feeding time arrived—Elena felt remarkably well, all things considered, and was sure when she walked, her feet never even touched the ground.

Oswolf performed the christening on the day after the birth, where the boy was given his true, Christian name. Elena had been calling him John for months now, but nobody saw fit to ask her opinion on the matter. The boy took the matter in stride, looking around at all the gathered faces without complaint, and once Oswolf poured the holy water over John's head and performed the sign of the Cross, he burped.

The body of the murdered king was set to be buried with great fanfare a full month after its discovery. The trip to Shaftesbury Abbey took most of the morning—Elena rode with Hugh, with John between them, tucked against her chest while wrapped in a thin blanket; the future Lord of Corfe was sleeping off a full belly, his warm cheek resting near her breast. She was still a bit tender in places, but most of the regular post-labor bleeding had slowed to a trickle or stopped entirely, and it felt like a necessary evil that she should go and witness the funeral in person. Elena needed to do it, to finally close that sordid chapter of her life for good.

Oswolf rode on one side, while Sybil rode on the other. The maidservant's face was a tightened mask of displeasure, reins clutched in her white knuckles.

"Are y'all right, lass?" the Scot asked.

Sybil mumbled something under her breath and shifted in her stirrups for the tenth time in half as many minutes. Elena saw the woman's jaw clenching. "I'm just not feeling well today."

"Aye?" Oswolf's eyebrows went up. "An' what seems t'be ailin' ye?"

It was hard to see, but to Elena, it looked as though Sybil's face was becoming flushed. She wriggled in the saddle again, mumbling something under her breath.

Oswolf raised a hand to her ear. "What's that?"

The maidservant rolled her eyes. "I do not handle horseback riding well. You know that well enough."

"I dinnae see why," he said. "Y'seem t'do well enough at't—ridin', I mean."

Sybil said something under her breath, sounding more irritable by the second, but Elena couldn't pick it out.

"Say again, lass. M'a wee bit hard o'hearin' today."

"Oh, for the love of... I said my ass is sore!" Sybil's voice cracked as she said it, as if speaking the truth aloud caused her physical pain.

The Lord and Lady looked at Sybil at the same time, then over to Oswolf in the same manner.

Oswolf hesitated for a second. "Ah."

"Nothing you weren't *already* aware of, I might add," Sybil said next, glaring over at Oswolf. Then she seemed to think better of her statement, went pale, and hunched her shoulders up, sinking down in her seat like she wanted to shrivel up and disappear.

Hugh turned his head, looking back at Elena. Elena looked back, eyebrows nearly up to her hairline, mouth opened, yet unsure of what to say.

The priest started to answer right away, then seemed to think better of it for a long, awkward moment. "Ah, m'sympathies. I should'a known better than t'go buttin' in like that."

"I don't know, Os," Hugh said, his face as passive as Elena had ever seen it. "I think you enjoy the occasional butt, sometimes."

Elena saw something she'd never seen before. Oswolf *blushed*. She cleared her throat, checking to make sure the baby was still asleep. "Why are you so sore, Sybil?"

"Ask *him*," Sybil said in a sulking, petulant manner, then obviously thought better of it when she added, "Milady."

Swiveling her head to the other side, Elena looked over to the giant Scot next. "Oswolf?"

Oswolf, never one to be at a loss for words before, appeared to be struggling with a response. He looked over at Sybil, who refused to look back at him. "Ah... well, lass—er, Milady—the thing t'understand is I... M'not sure how t'put this, but..." He cleared his throat, looking over at Sybil and back again several times. "Sybil an' m'self... We both happened to be... well..."

"Oh, *shut up*, you over-sized, wool-headed, cassock-wearing jackass," Sybil growled. She covered her face with both hands, shaking her head with a sad-sounding moan.

"So..." Hugh looked back and forth again, side to side. "Oswolf... You and Sybil?"

The Scot scratched his neck, coughed several times, cleared his throat. "Aye, Hugh, we are. What of't?" He huffed and rolled back his shoulders, as though challenging the other man.

"Are what?" Elena said.

"Well... *involved*, I s'pose ye might say," Oswolf said.

"God, just kill me now," Sybil said, muffled, into her hands.

"For how long?"

The priest squinted at the sky, counting off on his fingers. "A year? I think?"

"A whole *year*?" Elena looked at Sybil in disbelief. "And you never *told* me?"

"'Twas at my request, y'understand," Oswolf interjected.

"Please, Great Lord," Sybil said, looking Heavenward. "One bolt of lightning, that's all I ask."

"All right, all right," Hugh said, raising a hand on either side for silence. "There'll be time to discuss this later, and it *will* be discussed. Rest assured of that." He looked to either side, fixing each of them with a long, hard look.

"Yes, Lord," Sybil said, looking as though she still wished for a quick death.

Oswolf sniffed, scrubbing under his nose. "Aye, Milord."

Hugh seemed satisfied with that and tucked his heels in, urging his horse to a canter, forcing the other two to keep up.

∼

THE FUNERAL for King Edward was a far more grand, ostentatious and formal affair than his first had been. Although the body was moved in secret, a grand procession had set out a month later, taking a full week's time to walk from Wareham to the Abbey, overseen by Dunstan personally. A crowd had followed the procession, and according to what Elena heard later, great signs and portents occurred during the march north. Inside the Abbey itself, Edward would be laid to rest with honor, with his sepulcher prepared to rest just north of the central altar.

Two years prior, Elena, Hugh and Oswolf stood in a rain-soaked graveyard, and the parish priest spoke a short, if honest, prayer for the fate of Edward's soul. Now, Shaftesbury Abbey was packed full of mourners, onlookers, royal hangers-on and much more. Elena wondered how many of the people there were the ones calling Edward a saint, and just how the news of his uncorrupted corpse would affect that, ready to spread like a fire in a sea of dry grass. But then, she supposed that was how all cults started.

The Abbey was full to bursting and the crowd overflowed out into the yard, with people crammed up next to every available opening, straining to hear what went on inside. It was impossible not to draw parallels between Edward's funeral and the one of his father, Edgar, whose funeral Elena had also attended years earlier at Glastonbury Abbey. Then and now, that church was full of people; then and now, Dunstan was officiating. He had supported Edgar in life, and when Edgar died, supported Edward's claim to the throne next. The Archbishop looked very thin on the dais, standing over the coffin which contained Edward's body, already sealed in hopes of protecting the body from any further chance at decay, now that it had been taken out of the earth and moved elsewhere.

The Abbess, a short woman who ran the abbey, clad completely in severe black, stood a short distance from the altar, near to Ealdorman Elfhar. Elfhar's man, Ivan Black-Neck, was not in attendance. Hugh, as Ealdorman of Dorsetshire, stood next to Elfhar to observe the proceedings, while Oswolf stood close-by with Elena and Sybil, as well as other citizens of Corfe who'd made the journey to attend the ceremony. What Elena didn't expect was that no one from Æthelred's court—not the King or the Queen Regent, not even a representative—would attend. She remembered Edward being fond of his younger brother, and somehow longing for affection from his step-mother, but those feelings appeared to have been only one-sided, at best. That struck her as very sad, somehow. One last time, Edward was being cheated out of the affection he'd longed for in life. Now, in death, there was nothing left for him.

"Gathered host," Dunstan said, raising his voice to quiet the throng. "Abbess, Lords, Ladies, my good people... Years ago, I was privileged to speak at the final rites for King Edgar, whose reign was tragically cut short in the prime of his youth. Now, it is my sad duty to repeat that performance again over the body of his son, Edward, who too was cut down before his time. Youth is, as many of us know, wasted on the young." The sight of a smile on Dunstan's face just looked wrong to Elena—too thin, too unnatural, like the man himself. "But," he continued, "when youthful life is ended prematurely... such a tragedy is one to be mourned, and is felt amongst all of us.

"King Edward could have been great—his rule would have, I'm sure, taken our land to heights unforeseen and unknowable. At Edgar's funeral, I spoke of looking to the past, present, and the future ahead of us. Would that we had listened, and when the dark path lay ahead, deviated from that path, and the events that brought us to this sad, sad day." Elena heard several *amens* in the crowd about her. "Edward was, without a doubt, one of the greatest men who ever walked amongst us, and the loss of him... we feel as one people. We mourn him, grieve him—surely, he was worth more than the sad, shameful end he was forced to endure."

Sybil, standing behind Elena, was cradling the sleeping John to her chest, gently swaying back and forth to soothe him. The two women locked eyes for a moment. Sybil was there, had seen what Edward's beating did to her—Sybil had seen the scars Elena carried on her back when she'd attended to Elena's labor, just days earlier.

"To God, we commend the spirit of our fallen King. We thank God for the miraculous sign that young Edward granted us, even unto death, and we pray that God may take Edward's spirit unto Him. Amen."

Another loud chorus of *amens* responded to Dunstan's prayer, and those praying made the sign of the Cross.

In the silent moment thereafter, Elena silently forgave Edward for his crimes, for the violence he'd visited on her. After two years, she didn't want to hold onto resentment for him any longer. And, in a manner of speaking, it was possible that if not for her time meeting Edward, at becoming wrapped up in some way with the question of who should succeed King Edgar, she and Hugh might not have reconciled, and John might have never been conceived at all. So she whispered her own prayer for the dead young man, then turned and gently took John back, cradling him lovingly, gently shushing him when he whimpered. She pressed her mouth to his head, breathing in the smell of him, kissing his tuft of black hair.

So Edward was laid to rest, drawing his story to a close—at least, as far as Elena was concerned. If more was to transpire afterwards, she wanted no part of it.

As the crowd began to disperse, John began rooting and searching, needing to feed. Elena withdrew with Sybil, finding a private alcove where she could nurse in peace and quiet. Of course, if there was anywhere that had to be safe enough for a pair of women to be alone, they could do worse than an abbey.

For a time, all Elena heard was the hum of the crowd as it continued filing out the doors; their part in that particular play was over. But others remained behind, it seemed. She heard footsteps on the stones nearby, heard the familiar voice of her husband approaching. "Shouldn't blame yourself."

Elena caught Sybil's eye, urged her to step back and raised a finger to her lips. Sybil nodded, stepping away from the opening to take a seat next to her.

There was a sigh. "Yet, Hugh, I still feel some blame, all the same." Elena recognized the voice as Elfhar's. "You supported Edward's claim, at first; I thought his brother would be the better choice, and said so openly. Time will tell as to which of us was right, but I can only pray the events that led to today will help to right any wrongs I may have done to him in life. I thank you, if not for your wife's suggestion and your offer of Shaftes-bury, I'm not sure I would have had the chance to atone at all."

There was the sound of flesh slapping flesh—a soft sound, as one hand clasps another. "It was my pleasure, Lord Elfhar. But, now I must make a confession, as well."

"A confession? From you?" Elfhar laughed. "Have I been played somehow?"

If she knew Hugh, he was shaking his head. "Nay, Lord. But the matter is a sensitive one. Should we find somewhere more private?"

Both women looked at each other, and Sybil's eyes went wide. It wasn't likely that Elfhar would appreciate their eaves-dropping, not to mention Hugh's disapproval. The maid opened her mouth to speak when Elfhar cut her off. "No, I think this place should serve well enough—if a House of God isn't safe for us to speak within, what place is?"

Elena took the opportunity to switch John from one breast to the other, better to keep him quiet and content for as long as possible.

"Shouldn't we speak up, Milady?" Sybil whispered, hardly more than a breath, against Elena's ear.

"We should, but we won't," Elena answered. This had to be

the moment Hugh would bring up the subject of Corfe—she hadn't dared to dream she'd be fortunate enough to hear of it without her husband's invitation to sit in on the proceedings. "Hush now."

"Speak then," Elfhar said.

Hugh didn't waste time mincing words. "You're aware of the Danish raids this year? Chestershire. Tanet. Rochester. Southampton."

"I am. Chestershire falls within Mercia's borders, after all." Elfhar sighed. "A sad portent of the future, to be sure. Already I've had Ivan and others in my employ working at shoring up my coastal defenses."

"It's in that matter where I require assistance, Lord," Hugh said, jumping right to the point. "The Danes who attacked Tanet were either sheltered or helped by Count Richard of Normandy; I suspect the others received similar support, though I've been unable to confirm that yet. Corfe lies almost direct across the sea from the Norman port at Cherbourg—that my people have evaded attack so far might be the work of none less than God Himself, but now I must trust my people's fate to men. I have need of swords and strong arms to carry them."

"And you believe I can provide them?" Elfhar's voice was neutral, yet intrigued. "Why not go to the King and his mother? Surely they have enough strength of arms to defend you."

"They may, Lord, but Elfrida has a long arm and a longer memory. As you said, I supported the elder of Edgar's sons for the throne. The Queen remembers that, and I believe she would sooner see me gelded before her son's court than to provide the support I require."

"I would not care to make an enemy of Æthelred, Hugh," Elfhar said, sounding concerned. "Nor especially of his mother."

"Nor I," Hugh agreed. "But the boy-king will become a man, someday; he won't dance on strings forever. I must see to my defenses now, and seek forgiveness in the proper time."

There was a long pause. John squirmed and lost his grip on the nipple he was feeding from. Elena shushed him as softly as she could and put him back into place, praying the men would say their piece and move on before the boy started fussing in earnest.

"And," Hugh continued, as though seizing on Elfhar's hesitation, "it would only be in the case of any actual attack. Should the Danes return to their waters and seek better hunting elsewhere, you would simply be out the time and expense to supply a host of soldiers that were never even needed—an expense I would certainly repay in kind."

There was another long pause. Elena felt Sybil next to her, stiff as a wooden post. As for herself, she hardly dared to breathe.

"Cunning and shrewd as ever, Isarnon," Elfhar said, but Elena thought she heard the hint of a smile in his voice. "Perhaps it was too trusting of me to accept your offer of Shaftesbury without looking for any angle you might've been playing on the side."

Elena expected her husband to refute such words, but he did no such thing. "To have the 'prince of Mercia' in my debt was indeed a prize I coveted, Lord," Hugh said. "Yet, would you have done any less for your people had our roles been reversed?"

"No," Elfhar admitted with a chuckle, "I suppose not, at that. But don't think that Elfhar of Mercia is a prize so easily won, Lord Iron Hand." Elena could almost hear the smug grin in the man's voice. Either Hugh had nothing to say, or urged the other nobleman to continue. "What do you know of Brycheiniog and Morgannwg?"

"Welsh provinces," Hugh said, "or kingdoms, depending on who's asking. The last king of Morgannwg, Owain ap Morgan, left the region to his four sons—Rhys, Ithel, Hywel and Iestyn, all trying to share the crown together. Meanwhile, Brycheiniog keeps getting passed around from one Welsh lord to another like a communal mug in an alehouse."

"You've family there, haven't you?" Elfhar said.

"Mostly distant relations," Hugh said. "My grandmother, Branwen, was born in Talgart, Brycheiniog's largest town."

"So you know the region." It was a leading question, so obvious a blind man would have seen it.

Hugh grunted. "Well enough, I suppose."

"Well, those four brother-kings—such as they are—are either stretching their muscles or they lack the ability to keep some of their more-eager soldiers in line. They've been spotted crossing over into Mercia and causing all sorts of havoc. My man Ivan, when he finds the time, is building up a force for a counter-offensive to march into Brycheiniog later on this spring. I could make use of a man of your martial experience in that... in exchange for shoring up Corfe's defenses when the time is right, of course."

"A trade, then."

"Precisely," Elfhar said with satisfaction. "You march with my force for a tour, cross over into Wales and show them that Mercia isn't to be trifled with and I, in turn, will see that Corfe and Dorset County has the men it needs."

Elena felt her stomach melt down into her shoes. She nearly jumped to her feet and stomped out to shout her disapproval of any such plan, but Sybil's tight hold of Elena's arm stopped that. Instead, the Lady could only listen to her husband, praying he would refuse, knowing he had no such option—Elfhar had him to rights, and they all knew it.

"My wife..." Hugh spoke slowly, displeasure in his voice. "She will disapprove. My son was born just a short time ago, and I'm loath to leave them so soon."

"I understand," Elfhar said. "But, if it assuages your conscience at all, the campaign isn't set to start for another few weeks, a month or more at least. I'm returning to Tamworth on the morrow, but shall await you there. If I see you, that shall be answer enough, wouldn't you say? And no hard feelings, whatever that answer might be, in return for the kindness you've done me today."

There was an endless, agonizing moment of silence. Then Hugh said, "Agreed."

"Splendid!" Elfhar clapped his hands. "We're in accord, then. With that out of the way, I think our bargain well struck. Walk with me, Lord. There are some final matters with Dunstan that need settling before we all go our separate ways."

The Iron Hand grunted his agreement, and the sound of footsteps started away. In moments they were gone, leaving the two women behind.

Elena could see Sybil looking at her, but she had nothing to say. She felt empty, angry and afraid at the same time. The thought of Hugh going off to war filled her with such an awful dread her heart felt ready to stop beating.

John, in the meantime, finished his meal, detached from the nipple in his mouth, and burped. Elena took that as a less than promising sign.

A PROMISE MADE

The ride from Shaftesbury to Corfe was one of the longer trips in recent memory for Elena. Her mind was ablaze with different, competing desires—wanting to speak to Sybil, wanting to talk to Hugh, wanting to scream with general frustration. John was irritable on the whole ride back, even after being changed, so focusing on him provided her with a distraction so she didn't have to come up with conversation, and it was a while before the boy finally fell asleep. Sybil and Oswolf rode together just behind the Lord's horse, having ceased their earlier bickering. If Elena hadn't been so distracted, she would've been hounding the two of them with questions. For now, those questions would have to wait.

It wasn't until they were finally home that there was any chance to talk to Hugh at all. The sun was nearly set when they rode into the Hall's main yard, and then there was too much happening to talk about much of anything. When they finally got inside, Elena laid the sleeping babe down in his tiny bed on the far side of their bedroom, in a shadowed corner away from any windows, and spun around to face her husband.

"I forbid it," she said, straightening her back and staring him down.

Hugh turned around from where he stood at their bedroom door and raised an eyebrow. "Forbid what, Wife?"

Elena stepped closer, speaking much more softly than she wanted to—her temper demanded she start shouting, given how the words had been burning in her brain all day, but better that she keep her voice down than having an argument while also trying to shush a screaming newborn. "The Ealdorman's demand that you go riding off to Wales, or Mercia, or to God-knows-where. It's unconscionable to ask such a thing of a man with a wife and a new baby at home."

"Good, then you were listening," he said as he locked their door for the night.

"And what's more, I—what?" She stared, mouth agape. "H-how did you know I was listening?"

The look he gave her was long, weighted with expectation. "Did you think we just happened to stop by that particular alcove by mere happenstance, Elena?"

Elena had, admittedly. She didn't say so aloud, though. "Why would you do that?"

"Because I know Elfhar. I warned you, men of his stature don't just stumble into power by accident. Elfhar was going to want something in return for my request. Better that you heard it from his own mouth than mine."

She nodded, dumbly, not knowing what to say.

"And since I *knew* you were listening," Hugh continued, "obviously that means you *have* to realize that Elfhar has me by the short hairs, and I'm not referring to my beard."

"A colorful summation, Husband," Elena said, wrinkling her nose.

"And God's own truth," Hugh said. He reached over, squeezing her shoulders, leaning down to look into her eyes. "What would you have me do, starling? Shall I refuse him?"

"Well..." Elena knew what her heart wanted, and nearly spoke it aloud. But the look on his face, the hard shine of his eyes, stopped her.

"Shall I go to Æthelred and Elfrida? Cast myself down before the royal seat? Plead for mercy and understanding, knowing that neither are likely to be granted to me?"

Elena let her head fall against his firm chest, closing her eyes. He smelled good, so unbelievably good, and she wanted to be angry at him for it. "Is there no other way?" she whispered.

He kissed the top of her head. "There's always another way," he said, gently. "But this time, I don't see it." He took her hands, drew her towards the bed. "The Danes *will* come. Corfe *will* need protection—trained soldiers I do not have and cannot pay for, nor raise on my own. I must see our home defended, or it *will* be overrun." Hugh sat her down on the edge of the bed, then took a seat next to her. "Æthelred won't send soldiers on his own, whether that be his choice or his mother's, I see no reason for their minds to change now. Elfhar has the means, and, after today, the incentive to assist us, so long as I pay the price he requires of me."

"But why must *you* pay anything?" Elena curled her hands into fists in her lap, felt the sting of her fingernails pressing into her palms. "Why now? John is here now. Can't you simply train our men in the village to fight?" She knew it was a selfish request, yet asked it anyhow.

"I can," he said, nodding, "but it would take months or more to train them properly, time I don't have to take them from their own lives, the families they provide for, the farms and other work they must do. And that means asking them to put their lives on hold, for all that time, and then asking them to face off against trained, hardened warriors and killers when they come to our shores." He paused, as though to let her consider that plan. "Or... I can give up my own desires, ask you to put aside yours for a season, give Elfhar what he wants, and then come back with the knowledge our home and its people will be protected, should we ever have need of it."

"But we've come so far," she said. "I thought we were done with kings and nobles, and prices having to be paid."

Hugh smiled, but it was sad at the edges—perhaps sad for her, if not for himself. "My poor, starling. Perhaps you may be right, one day, but I don't think it likely to happen anytime soon."

"Of course I'm right." She raised her head and blew out a breath of anger, of frustration at the whole affair. She took long, calming breaths after, taking his hand and pulling it into her lap. His fingers were warm, and felt good when interlaced with her own. "We still have time, though don't we?"

"Yes." Hugh's arm felt good around her shoulders as he pulled her close to him again, and she closed her eyes at the soft, repeated kisses he pressed atop the crown of her head. "For now, certainly for tonight, and another week at least. There'll need to be preparations made, people informed about my absence and such, but I won't just up and disappear with the dawn tomorrow morning."

She'd made a promise to herself, not too long ago, that she would do whatever she could to support him in his work, to lighten the load he was forced to carry. Now Elena had to follow through on that promise—a chance to prove to herself that she could manage things in his absence. It wouldn't be the first time, perhaps not even the hundredth, but it was very likely to be the longest. Part of her wanted to just shut out the world and ignore any talk of Danish invaders or Elfhar, or anything else for that matter, but what good would that do? Hugh depended on her. Hugh needed her to be willing to give up what she wanted for him, for the people who depended on both of them.

"All right," Elena said. "Then if I'm to agree to this, I have a list of demands that must be met first."

The look on Hugh's face was one of mild surprise. "Very well. Go on."

"First off, I expect the order to come down from you personally that I speak in your stead, and any decisions made are done in your stead, and obeyed as such."

"You didn't strike me as the tyrannical type, starling," Hugh said with a smile, albeit a small one.

"By my measurement, my Lord, we're less than two score years from the dawn of the 11th century. Sooner or later, men *will* have to follow a woman's orders, whether it be simply necessary or not." She raised an eyebrow. "Or do you not trust me to carry on your affairs in your absence, just as you've always done?"

"A fair point," he said, nodding. "All right, what else?"

"I-" Elena stood up, feeling flustered. "I don't... don't think you've ever made plans to be gone for this long." She stalked the room, pacing back and forth while talking in soft, clipped tones, waving her hands about as she did so. "I therefore *insist* we sit down and have a proper meeting with the rest of the staff to make them aware of this, and how best to handle the running of the Hall and addressing the needs of the townsfolk while you're away." She stopped and turned around to face him again. "Your authority must continue to be recognized during these trying times, my Lord."

"Most assuredly," Hugh answered.

Elena narrowed her eyes. "Are you jesting on my account, Husband?"

"Maybe a little."

She felt her hackles rise as she stopped in front of him, having run out of room in which to pace. "That seems to me *most* unnecessary, especially at a time like this."

"A time like what, Elena?"

"Well—"

"Listen to me." Hugh took her arms in his enormous hands,

squeezing them, pulling her nearly nose-to-nose with him. "I demand the best of our servants, of those who protect our house, of the people who reside in our town and call me their Lord. I expect *none* of that will change when I'm away, anymore than it changes anytime I go to Winchester or anywhere else on the King's business. Whether I'm gone for a week or a whole season is immaterial to me." He released his strong grip, sliding his hands up to cup her cheeks. "*You*, on the other hand, are not. I need your trust in this, starling. What I'm going to do is for us and our son, more so than for anyone else here. Can you understand that?"

"No," she said without thinking, felt her cheeks go warm when it slipped out. She looked down, felt the urge to cry, but fought it. Instead of crying, she took a hard sniff, looked in his eyes again. "But I can do my best to trust if you have to leave... you'll also come back."

"Starling—"

Elena cut him off, pressing her face to his, cutting off his words with a kiss. She kissed him hard, with sorrow at his having to leave, fear that he might not come back, and more than a month of pent-up physical need burning inside of her until she felt ready to break. She didn't want to break yet, there'd be time enough for that. Right now, he was what she wanted.

Hugh seemed surprised by the vigor and lust of her kisses, so much that it stole his breath away. He broke it to breathe a long moment later and looked up at her. "Is it... not too soon, then?"

She shook her head, pulling his shirt up, running her fingernails up over his broad shoulders and down his back, somehow finding enough breath between more kisses. "Isolda said four weeks would be long enough to wait. It was five weeks day before yesterday."

That appeared to be all the dispensation that Hugh required, given the sound of the growl in his throat, the way he pulled her to the bed and rolled over on top of her. It was so fast, so sudden and powerful and *hungry*, yet Elena laughed in surprise, only stifling herself at the last second by clapping a hand over her mouth. "Careful!" she hissed at him, feeling his hands in her skirts. "If you wake him up, *you* can stay up all night with him."

"He's not the one I'm interested in staying up with," Hugh said. The look on his face struck Elena as comical in a nonplussed, nonsensical sort of way and she had to choke back another urge to start laughing.

Hugh had her skirts up above her waist in one moment, and his pants down past his knees the next. It felt like how she imagined two young lovers might have acted, fumbling for belts and fabric in the dark, afraid at being discovered if they wasted too much time. But then, they had their own eavesdropper now, and wasting too much time might ruin any chance at intimacy—that was definitely going to take some getting used to.

The weight of her husband's body was welcome and familiar to her, and Elena smothered her gasp and moan against his neck as he entered her. "Gently," she whimpered, pleading—she didn't expect him to do anything that would harm her, he was too careful for that, but she still didn't know how she might react to physical intimacy. Thankfully, her lover was a tender sort and took his time, plying her with warm, bristling kisses and fingers curled snug into her thick brown hair as he moved again, more gently. He was more patient than she expected, taking just enough time considering the hasty manner of their reunion, knowing at any moment the spell could break with the sound of a newborn's cry.

Propping her legs up on either side of him, Elena's fears proved unnecessary, and she sighed with contentment and new happiness. She'd missed this feeling, the way he held her with such a jealous love. When she didn't cry out or protest, Hugh seemed to take that as a sign he could continue with greater gusto, and she was glad he did. In moments she was clutching his shirt tight in her fingers, rolling her head back, breathing deep through her opened mouth. Having her husband on top of her, inside of her, becoming one with her was the greatest thing in her entire world. Elena had missed it, terribly—she loved her son as much as any mother could, but her love for Hugh Isarnon was something altogether different. It felt like comparing the light of a burning torch to that of a glowing iron, pulled out of a fire: both of them would burn her, both of them were hard to look upon for more than a few moments, but one had left its permanent mark on her soul as surely as a brand scarring her living flesh.

The man's thrusting rhythm picked up a faster pace, and Elena rolled her head to one side, welcoming his hot, wet kisses to her chin and throat, drinking in the sensation of his breathing as it poured over her bared flesh. She pulled the neckline of her dress open wider, letting him feast on the sight of her breasts with his eyes; looking up at him through her lashes, she cupped them, knowing how he loved looking at her and touching her, becoming a tease for his senses. When she licked her lips, it broke him—she watched his face go tight, his eyes nearly closed, and felt how hard he pushed up inside of her one last time. The pulsing, liquid sensation of his muscles flexing and moving within her, the feel of his seed being poured into her, filled her with a satisfaction not unlike an orgasm of a different kind. She had pleased him, and that was a satisfaction all its own.

Her lover took a long, long moment to catch his breath. When he rolled off of her, over to one side and onto his back, she stayed on hers, looking up at the dark ceiling over their heads. She found his hand, grabbed it, squeezed it tight.

Hugh took another breath, raised her hand to his lips. "Thank you," he said, still winded.

Elena slowly pushed up to both elbows, looking across the room. Compelled to check on John, she stood up and slipped over to his crib to check on him, but the little one slept on, quiet for the moment, undisturbed by the amorous activities of his parents.

When she returned, Hugh was still lying there half-dressed, but now he was watching her, eyes shining in the dark. She stopped at the side of the bed, looking him over with pursed lips, then found his eyes again. "It seems to me we still have some time left tonight, my Lord."

He smiled, pushing up to a seated position. "Then perhaps we should do something about that."

So they did.

LATER—ELENA had no idea how late it was—they were curled up together in bed in the manner she approved of most, her back to his chest, his arms wrapped around her, his warm breath in her hair.

"You *will* be careful won't you, Hugh?" Her eyes hurt, yet she didn't want to close them, knowing she wasn't likely to get much sleep once the baby woke up for his next feeding.

"I'm always careful, Elena," he said.

"No." She spun around in bed, taking his face in her hands. Such a fire was in her eyes, lit up with such fervent emotion and fear the whole room should have burst into flames. "Promise me, Hugh. I *need* to hear it. If you... if you didn't come back, I don't... I..." Her mouth was suddenly dry, as though she'd crammed a mouthful of sand into it. Her aching eyes were burning, but she didn't look away.

Hugh rested a hand atop her head, and didn't flinch away from her stare. "Starling, you can't—"

"No!" Elena raised her voice, unable to stop herself, not wanting to. She rose onto both knees, leaning over him. She grabbed his shoulders, wanting to shake him until all of the teeth rattled inside his big, beautiful head. "I don't *want* to hear anything else. Promise me, damn you."

He still didn't flinch. Elena wasn't sure how she would've reacted if he had. "I promise, Elena. I *will* be careful. I *will* come back to you. As God above and you are my witnesses, I swear it."

There was a rustling sound at the other side of the room, as if John had jumped or been startled in his sleep by his mother's outcry, but after a moment of tiny whimpers, he went quiet again.

Wife and husband, Lady and Lord, they both stared at one another, not moving, neither of them willing to break the gaze of the other. Finally, she relented and slowly, deliberately, slid back under the covers and nestled up to him again, taking her old position back as if nothing had happened. But when his arm slid around her, pulled her back tight to his chest, Elena's weak resistance crumbled and she began to cry. Hugh had no words of comfort, no gentle lies to tell her, so he held her tight as she pressed the pillow to her mouth to silence her sobs.

After several minutes she was exhausted, and had no energy left for tears. With the feeling of his breath and silent kisses in her hair, Elena closed her eyes and took what sleep she could find, knowing that more tears would come in time.

A TIME APART

*I*t was a warm, rainy day in late April when Hugh Isarnon departed his home with a small escort and headed north. Elena insisted on watching him go, a thick shawl pulled over her head, standing at the gate while she watched his dark shape vanish into the mist. Her scarred back burned with a terrible, mournful sort of pain. It was a sad day, and her heart ached from feeling so heavy, but she stood and waited for a long time after he was out of sight—she knew he was gone, but also wouldn't forgive herself if he'd somehow turned around and didn't find her still waiting for him.

That wasn't the first time the Lord of Corfe had taken his leave and left his wife behind to care for his home and his people. The job of an ealdorman meant Hugh was often required to travel on his business, or the King's. Although the royal court was generally located in the town of Winchester, which in itself was a two or three day journey on horseback, it was the habit of England's kings to roam about and settle down wherever they pleased, be it at Winchester, Lunden, Canterbury or elsewhere, which sometimes required the Iron Hand to go riding or sailing all over half the countryside just to get anything done. One surprising, unexpected development was Oswolf didn't accompany Hugh on his latest journey. Elena felt certain the Scot disapproved of Hugh leaving him behind, but he didn't complain or make a fuss about it, either.

Life at home continued. With no way to send word as to his whereabouts and very little chance of him coming home anytime soon, Elena bore his absence as best she could. John required a great deal of time and attention, in-between regular feedings, too-infrequent naps and the general neediness that any baby would have. It became the lady's habit to sneak whatever catnaps she could find whenever she could find them—those first few weeks she felt like some unholy creature constantly walking around in a daze. Sybil and Isolda's help was invaluable during that time, and they sometimes spoke with the full authority of their Lady—any man with enough sense kept any unnecessary questions to himself, and those with less sense learned not to ask questions more than once.

One thing Elena handled almost immediately after Hugh's departure was the matter of Sybil and Oswolf. She never saw a man squirm so much as he did in his chair after she sat them down and asked the obvious question, "Why were you keeping your relationship a secret from Hugh and me?" John was in Elena's lap at the moment, lying on his back and attempting— with some gusto—to fold himself in half. The future Lord of Corfe had developed a strange fascination with his own toes and kept trying to jam them into his mouth, usually with only a modicum of success.

For her part, Sybil looked down and didn't say anything. It wasn't that she seemed particularly ashamed to Elena's eye, but preferred to let Oswolf do the talking first.

To say Oswolf looked uncomfortable was a gross understatement. "Well, lass, I-I s'pose as that t'would depend on yer meanin' o'the word 'secret,' ye ken."

Elena pursed her lips for a moment. "So, to ask it another

way, were you deliberately obfuscating your romantic intent towards my personal maidservant and the keeper of my house, Father?"

Oswolf was quiet, as if weighing his words carefully.

"Iffin' ye follow mah meanin', I s'pose," Elena added in her best, or perhaps worst, impression of the man's brogue.

Sybil barked a laugh of surprise, pressing a hand across her mouth to stifle it. Oswolf visibly winced. "Pray, Elena, iffin' ye have *any* affection fer me left, dinnae do that e'er again. Please."

The lady adjusted the newborn on her lap, wiping his drooling mouth clean on a spare towel she had tied at her waist. "Answer the question, Oswolf."

The Scot sighed and looked over at Sybil. "'Twas on account o'the bairn, ye see."

Elena raised an eyebrow. "John?"

"A'fore he was born, aye," Oswolf said. "Things got good'n serious 'tween Sybil'n m'self 'round the time ye and Hugh made yer announcement, and we didnae think it would've been... say, the *proper time* an' all, t'go seekin' yer blessin' on the matter."

"So you decided to keep waiting until the 'proper time' just happened to come along? And an entire *year* happened to pass in the meantime?"

Oswolf visibly winced. "I'll grant ye, perhaps, that I might 'ave planned t'speak of't a wee bit more strategically than that."

"Perhaps, Father, you might have indeed done that," Elena answered, fixing him with a long look. Looking to Sybil next, she softened her voice. "Were you afraid or ashamed to speak of it with me?"

"No, Milady," Sybil answered, shaking her head. "It just... never felt like the right time to bring it up."

Elena took a long, slow breath as she looked from one face to the other. Sybil seemed resigned, withdrawn; Oswolf, uncertain but making a brave show of it anyhow.

"Oswolf."

"Mm?" He sat up a little straighter in his seat.

"You're aware Sybil has no living parents nor siblings to speak for her, yes?" Saying so made Sybil flinch, to hear her lady in such blunt, plain terms. Elena reached out, squeezing the other woman's hand in sympathy, before sitting up again. Sybil took John from her, cradling the little boy for a moment with a small, sad smile on her face.

Oswolf nodded. "Aye, lass, that I am."

"Then in the lord's absence, and with no one else to do the job, *I* shall speak for her."

"You, Elena?"

"And why not? If your intentions are honorable, what does it matter whether Hugh or I speak on Sybil's behalf?"

"Honorable?" The priest gave a mighty huff, which for him sounded like the far-away thrum of a thunderstorm. "Now look 'ere, this's nae some sort'f...of *dalliance*, nor an *amusement* t'wile away the time as't suits me. I ken that y'might've been surprised t'hear about our interest wit' one another, but m'intentions've ne'er been anythin' *but* honorable. M'a man o'God, after all—I would'nae dare t'think o'treatin' Sybil otherwise."

"Very well," Elena said with a nod. "Then when is the wedding?"

Sybil, still not speaking, gave a start but didn't drop the baby, thankfully. The look she gave Elena was a little wide-eyed, however.

To his credit, Oswolf didn't flinch. "Well, seein' as yer an interested party now'n all, I *was* plannin' t'ask Hugh what proper-like when 'e got back from 'is errands, ye ken." The man gave a scowl and, as though not knowing what else to do, he reached a hand to the woman seated next to him. Sybil's hand looked very small in his, but the maidservant smiled, none-theless. "D'ye propose any sort'f alternative, Milady?"

Elena took John back before he wiggled off of the other woman's lap. John had a mouthful of toes by that time and he squawked with distress when they were taken away from him. "Not at all—not so long as it doesn't interfere with Sybil's duties," she said, wiping her son's mouth clean again. "Or yours, I suppose," she added.

Oswolf nodded, as though satisfied by that answer.

"You *are* taking preventative measures, yes?" she said, giving Sybil a knowing look.

Sybil nodded. "Isolda recommended regular use of angelica herb, Milady. We, ah..." She looked at Oswolf and turned several shades of crimson at the same time, taking her hand back to tuck them both into her lap. "We're being quite careful. I wanted to tell you directly more than once, I truly did, but..." Her voice fell away for a moment. She cleared her throat. "As we said, I guess the time never felt... quite right." She gave a self-conscious smile and tucked some of her dark hair back.

"It never is, I suppose." Elena smiled back. "Oswolf could tell you a few stories about my husband and me—there were plenty of times I *never* knew the right time to say anything to him."

"Understatement of m'lifetime," Oswolf huffed, half-under his breath.

Sybil kicked his shin under the table.

"Gah!" The Scot hissed in pain and turned to one side with a wince. "Confound't woman, are y'daft? Whatever'd ye do that fer?"

Elena and Sybil shared a look, as though nothing else needed to be said.

Time passed.

The rainy days of spring turned into the warm, sweltering days of summer. Elena was ignorant in the ways of war, or whatever it was Hugh was involved in—she couldn't begin to imagine where he might be or what he was doing. She cried, of course.

Oh, how she cried. Sometimes she wondered if this was how a new bride felt, if she had any right to be so despondent at Hugh having to go away, if it wasn't somehow selfish of her to want him to come back. But Elena didn't care. After the first month, she wasn't crying herself to sleep every night, but there were more teary-eyed days than clear-eyed ones.

Every single morning, Elena woke with an empty hole in her heart and in her bed that nothing could fill up until Hugh came home; every night, when she had time for sleep, she'd lie alone in that same bed and whisper into the dark, willing the words to somehow be carried away on an unfelt wind all the way to wherever her husband was. Elena spoke of John and how every week, sometimes every day, brought some new discovery. Elena had been an only child and orphaned early, besides—motherhood was an exciting, terrifying thing to experience, and if not for wiser and cooler heads than hers, she might've gone out of her mind with panic on some days. By his third month, John was already teaching himself to roll over; a month later, he once rolled himself all the way over to one wall of his mother's bedroom and managed to squirm his way underneath one of the tapestries hanging there—for a fleeting moment, she nearly flew into a conniption when she lost track of him, only to find one of his chubby legs sticking out, wiggling about as he babbled and fussed in consternation.

The worst part of it was the physical loneliness. Some days, and nights especially, her body cried out for her lost love, filling her with such a craving and sense of desolation that she wanted to scream. Lying in the dark, her legs apart, fingers between her thighs and a pillow pressed to her mouth to stifle her sounds, she sought satisfaction, relief, anything that could soothe the burning heat between her aching thighs. At times Elena felt so sensitive that she could barely manage to touch herself without sparks flashing in her eyes and her chest tightening up, but no amount of gentle caresses or quick, flickering touches would soothe that fire. She gritted her teeth, she tensed her muscles, she whispered or cursed Hugh's name—nothing worked. Finally, touched with sweat, aching with frustration, she gave up, and didn't have the heart to try again.

By the sixth month of Hugh's long journey, his son was starting to crawl—or, to put it more adequately, shuffle—his way across any flat surface he was granted access to. His nursing schedule slowed down as, with some reluctance, solid food was being introduced into his diet. This caused the young man to fuss incessantly, and on some evenings Elena had little gumption left in her to fight him. Nursing calmed the boy down, and on one particular evening she sat on a wooden bench next to his bed, cradling him as best she could as he supped. The air was heavy with moisture from an all-day, late October rain, as dark and depressing a day as Elena could remember for months. John had grown considerably longer and heavier, and Elena sometimes struggled with finding a comfortable position to hold him; her aching back did very little to help that. The boy's eyelids were heavy with sleep already, and Elena counted herself as incredibly fortunate that he was a deep and unusually heavy sleeper. The trade-off was the healthy set of lungs he possessed, and how he still enjoyed waking her up at odd hours of the night.

When it felt safe enough, Elena broke the seal of his sleeping suckling, tucked herself back into her dress and laid the boy down in his crib. Taking her seat again, she crossed her arms over her lap and leaned over him, watching his round face, brushing her fingers over the hair that had only thickened out and somehow darkened even more in the months since his birth. It became her nighttime ritual, before she turned in, to watch him sleep by the candlelight and make sure he was still breathing before she went to bed.

Elena felt a presence behind her and sighed, tucking the blankets around the little boy's sleeping form. "I love him, Sybil," she said. It was a compulsion, as instinctive as taking a breath. "I can't help myself. He's just so..." She sighed again. "So wonderful."

"That's good to hear."

It took half a breath—half a heartbeat—for Elena to recognize that voice, and she turned and flung herself at the speaker in one motion. Hugh caught her in his arms, and also managed to catch the bench, she'd toppled over, with the toe of his boot before it hit the floor and startled the baby awake.

"Gently, starling, gently," he said, cooing to her as he set the bench upright again.

"Shut *up*," she answered, squeezing her arms tighter around him. He was soaked—his clothes were dripping, to the point a thin pool was growing under his boots. His hair was soaked to the scalp, and his beard was studded with raindrops like clear gems. In moments, she was damp, but Elena only cared about kissing him over and over. Her eyes stung with happy, joyful tears. Minutes passed where nothing was said, nothing seemed to move or stir at all except for the silent flickering of the candles, John's heavy breaths, the sound of the rain falling outside, and the rainwater dripping off of Hugh's sodden clothes. She pressed her face tight into his chest, turning just enough so she could breathe, and didn't care that he stank of horse, wet flesh and old clothes.

"*You—*"Elena had to sniff, wipe her face and mouth dry with her towel."—need a bath, my lord."

"And a week's worth of sleep to catch up on," he said, taking a seat with a heavy sigh, closing his eyes for a long moment to catch his breath. He sounded tired. He sounded old, worn and wrung out, like a threadbare washcloth.

"Not to mention how you insist on sneaking in like some kind of miscreant to catch me unaware."

"A man has to find his pleasures where he can find them," he said, a tired but content smile on his face.

Elena heard a cough at the door, saw Sybil standing there, hands folded in front of her.

"Sybil," Elena said, "can you fetch the tub and—"

"Already on the way, Milady," Sybil said. As she said so, two men carried in the large wooden tub, setting it up next to the bed. "I'll have it filled shortly, and dinner for the lord as well. Will there be anything else?"

"No, Sybil." Elena shook her head and smiled. "Thank you."

"Of course." Sybil smiled back. "Welcome home, Milord."

"Thank you, Sybil," Hugh said, grunting again as he started pulling at his wet clothes with some effort. "Did Oswolf make an honest woman out of you yet?"

Sybil blushed, opening her mouth for a moment before finally finding the words to go with it. "We, ah... hoped to receive your blessing upon your return, you understand."

"You have it," he said, as his cloak dropped to the floor with a heavy, splatting sound. "Tell him I said to stop dragging his giant Scottish ass and get it done before I marry you off to someone else."

"Y-yes, Lord." Sybil was still blushing, but she was openly smiling, too.

Elena had a suspicion that Oswolf's days of freedom were numbered. For some reason, she approved of that.

A SWEET HOMECOMING

*T*here was no sweeter sound to Elena's ears than when Sybil bid her lord and lady goodnight and shut the door. She locked the door with Hugh's key and hung it in its place on the wall, and by that time, Hugh had already stripped out of his soaked breeches and was slowly climbing into the tub.

That was when she finally spotted it, a round patch of pale, scarred flesh as long as her thumb below his stomach on the left side, near his hip bone. "What's that?"

Hugh paused for a second on his way down, saw her face, then eased the rest of the way into the hot water. It smelled of dried lavender and had flower petals floating in it, leaving a faint, pleasant fragrance in the air. "What's what, starling?" he asked, leaning his head back and closing his eyes for a moment. He seemed absolutely exhausted, but that was no surprise, not knowing how far or how long he'd insisted on riding through rain and darkness to reach home.

"That scar, the new one on your left side."

He paused for a moment, opening one eye to look at her. "Scar?" His tone was just a touch too innocent, a shade too pure to be believed.

Elena dipped her chin and gave him a long look from beneath her eyebrows. "My lord, it has been my privilege, though perhaps not always my pleasure, to be your wife for thirteen years now, by my count. And whether through happenstance, necessity, obligation or simply on account of your, at times, *excessive* appetites, I should think I've seen every inch and then some of your person in a state of undress—can we agree on that?"

Hugh actually smirked—smug, handsome bastard that he was. "Likewise."

"Then we can agree if anyone knows your body well enough, it would be me. Correct?"

He nodded. "Indeed."

"So I will ask again. What. Is. That?" She pointed to the cloudy waters of the tub, towards his left-hand side. Her lips were pursed, eyebrows erect, waiting on his answer.

He considered her question for a moment, as though he were contemplating having to answer or not. He raised a finger, tilting his head purposefully. "I propose a trade, starling."

"A trade."

"Mm." He nodded, wagging the finger for emphasis. "I shall answer *your* question, if you will answer mine."

Elena crossed both arms at her stomach. "Very well. Ask away."

"Why exactly, if I've come so far to reach home and hearth tonight, and I have a tub large enough and warm enough for two people, are you not already in said tub keeping me company?" He looked up at her, plaintive and a little wistful.

It was such a strange, humorous look that Elena had to smile, no matter how she tried to fight the urge. "*That* is your question, Husband?"

"It is, Wife. I pray God will lead you to the correct answer."

"Oh—the *correct* answer, is it?"

"Truly." He nodded. "Surely there can be only one correct

answer as to why a man may be undressed and in a hot tub when his pretty wife is not."

"Indeed." She smiled. "And what answer *is* the correct one, pray tell?"

"Mm..." He squinted. "I'm sure it'll come to me. In the meantime, why not join me and we'll figure it out together?"

She sighed, looking down at herself—her clothes gone damp from holding him, and the room *was* a touch too chilly for its own good. "Sometimes it feels like I'm surrounded by children," she sighed with a touch of the dramatic, pulling the whole sodden mess of fabric up over her head. Hugh held his tongue, rather than respond to that, but his eyes were very, very interested in what he saw as she tossed her clothes into a heap on the floor and stepped into the tub with him. There was room enough for two, but it was comfortably snug as she sank into the water, sliding her shorter legs over his own as she gathered up her hair and let it hang over the side behind her. "Is this more to your liking, Hugh?" she asked.

"It is," he said, his voice softer now—deeper, more intense.

Elena wasn't above a bit of performance art, from time to time: she cupped the hot water, pouring it down one slender arm, rubbing the wet petals against her pale flesh, teasing him with the thing she knew he obviously wanted. Over her husband's shoulder, she could see the sleeping form of their son, see a bit of his round face still looking relaxed while he slept. "Now, seeing as I've tended to your question, perhaps you might tend to mine."

Hugh was looking over at the sleeping babe as well, and only turned back once she spoke. "Later," he said, less of a word, more like a hungry, disyllabic sound that she nevertheless understood all too well. When he reached for her, Elena didn't resist him— she supposed a part of her thought about it, contemplating resisting his advances until he fulfilled her demands and answered all of her questions, but a much, much larger part of her wanted something that couldn't be summed into words. She wanted to feel his flesh in her hands, to rake her nails over him until he bled; she wanted to feel him thicken in her mouth, to drink down every drop of sweet and salty nectar until she swelled with it. The touch of his flesh to hers was so hot Elena was sure there'd be scorch marks left behind. Such a tension was in him, every muscle gone taut, like a sprinter ready to break into a run at any moment. The touch of his hands on her arms was just short of painful, such pressure that made it feel like he might break her if he wasn't cautiously, deliberately careful... but he was also a man who'd returned home after almost half a year, and if his desire was anywhere near as strong as hers, Elena wondered how he was controlling himself at all.

Her wet hair clung to her back and around her shoulders, distracting her for a moment, but then his mouth pressed to hers and that distraction was forgotten. His teeth pressed tight around her lower lip, making her whimper into his mouth. He moved his hands down her back, into the water, cupping tight around both halves of her ass. The power in his fingers was delicious, and she wondered how many bruises he'd leave her with when the night was done.

They were of one mind together. He lifted her up while she reached down between them, finding his shaft already hard and ready; it throbbed in her fingers, twitching with violent and evident need. A moment passed between them as she looked down into his eyes, seeing how much he needed this—needed her—and holding back any longer might even cause him physical pain. Or maybe that was her need, reflected back at her in his eyes. Elena slid the swollen head into place and pushed down as hard as she dared. She pressed her mouth to the side of his neck to muffle her long, low cry of pleasure as they became one flesh again, fulfilling the desire she'd been unable to satisfy for far, far too long.

Water sloshed and splashed around them while she rode him,

savoring the feel of his cock inside of her, touching places she could never reach on her own. With one hand, she held onto his shoulder, digging her fingernails into his flesh to keep herself upright, while the other pressed tight to her belly, stretching her fingers down until she found her clit and started swirling around it, flicking the sensitive nub from side to side in the motion she knew would bring her to a quick end. The span of a few, lonely months seemed like it had lasted a lifetime, and neither she nor her lover wanted anything but quick, immediate relief.

Whether seconds or minutes long, the ride was arduous and physically taxing, but it was just as sweet as any prolonged, hour-long session of lovemaking could've been. Hugh rolled his head back and started to moan aloud, closing his mouth at the last possible second to keep the noise to a minimum, but he was already spent. The feeling of his cock swelling, pulsing, throbbing inside of her was intoxicating, just like always, and the sensation of him bursting within her swollen walls finally broke her just the way she wanted. Elena pushed down hard, grinding her aching bud against him, bone to bone, flesh against flesh; his bristling curls scratched against her mound with such exquisite pain it made her shiver.

Hugh wrapped his arms around her and crushed Elena to his chest. It wasn't a completely unpleasant sensation, but she did strain to breathe for just a second before he eased the pressure somewhat. "I missed you," he said.

"And I you," she answered, resting her head on his shoulder.

For several minutes, they floated there in the water, quiet and content, joined in flesh and spirit together. She hated the thought of breaking that bond, so Elena closed her eyes and remained still. He seemed to need her there, needing to know she was real. Hugh would occasionally press kisses to the crown of her head, as was his way, and Elena wouldn't have asked him to stop for the whole world.

Finally, as all loving moments must, that one came to an end, for Elena winced and whispered: "I, ah... think my legs are falling asleep."

"Here." There was scant room to maneuver, but after some slow and cautious adjustment, eventually she ended up in his lap, her back to his chest, his strong arms around her waist—it was a position he favored, and she didn't fight him. The heat of the water had fully soaked into his skin, replacing the cold, clammy feeling left behind by the rough weather he'd traveled in. For another moment he remained quiet, but let his head fall forward, resting his mouth on her shoulder; the gentle kiss he laid there was a sweet center at the middle of his scrubby, unkempt beard that bristled against her naked flesh. Elena closed her eyes and tried to memorize every sensation: the strength in his wide arms, the feel of his heavy legs and wide chest behind her, the touch of his breath across her neck and collarbone, the wonderful ache between her legs. She'd already shed her tears at their reunion, but now since he was home again, it served as a realization that, had things gone differently, he might not have come home at all.

"Hugh?" Elena's voice sounded sleepy in her own ears. She coughed, cleared her throat.

"Yes, dear."

"Please tell me how you got this." She reached down with her left hand, brushing in the vicinity of his left hip where she remembered seeing his scar. She kept her voice gentle—not wanting to pry, yet needing to.

When Hugh spoke, he spoke slowly, taking care in what he said and how vivid a picture he painted for her. "There was a skirmish, near a place called Archenfield—sometime in early June, I think. A Welsh spearman made a lucky thrust, got me in a bad way—nothing vital was hit, by some miracle, but I was down until Elfhar's men carried me from the field."

Elena stiffened, started to turn around, but he stopped her. "You were wounded? Why didn't you—"

"Elena, no, wait." He sighed, fingers at her cheek, urging her to turn just her head to look up at him. "We won that particular battle; the men fought bravely—they earned that victory and plenty others after it. I stayed to give Black-Neck and his soldiers what support I could before I had to quit the field. If I'd had proper time and treatment, it might not have left such a scar as it did." Hugh gave a tiny smile, shrugged one shoulder. "Just one more for the collection, I suppose."

"It was too heavy a price to pay," she said with venom in her voice. Now it was her turn to squeeze him tight, finally realizing just how close she'd come to losing him, and how she might have never known at all until it was too late. "But..." She sniffed, releasing her tight hold. "Thanks be you survived it. And now, I suppose, Elfhar will have to uphold his end of the bargain, if need arises."

"Yes." He set another kiss to the top of her head, something Elena approved of wholeheartedly. "It's too late in the year for raiding parties, I think if any of the Danes are this far from home, they'll be looking for somewhere to hole up for the winter, to wait out the cold months until spring."

"That's good, isn't it?" Elena permitted herself a moment of hopefulness. "They've stayed away this long, so..." She let her voice die away, unsure of what to say next.

"It is a good thing. But there've been other raids, both Cornwall and Exanceaster were attacked earlier this year, while I was away." His voice went softer, darker. "I won't trust to chance that we won't be next—it's only a matter of time now. I can feel it in my bones, starling, something bad is coming, and the sooner we're prepared to face it, the better."

Elena couldn't argue with that. Yet, she still hoped, deep in her heart of hearts, that the fate Hugh was prepared for might not come to pass after all.

AN HONEST PROPOSAL

*W*hen Hugh Isarnon called for a meeting of the Shire Court, the declaration was met with equal parts surprise and trepidation. The Court only met twice a year to handle important matters that affected the whole county, and the regularly scheduled meeting wasn't supposed to happen until early January, after the celebratory *Cristes Mæsse* holiday had come and gone. Every family in Dorsetshire was required to travel to Corfe, and every freeman over 12 years of age would be expected to attend. When the Iron Hand also declared any woman, who wished, would also be allowed to witness the meeting, more than a few of the more conservative-leaning citizens of the shire could be heard howling in protest, but it had the effect Hugh wanted. The promised attendance was more than double what he'd expected.

Over the next week, a makeshift tent city began to go up outside of Corfe. More and more joined their ranks every day, and by the night before the Shire Court, there was a veritable sea of white canvas on the hills around the town. Looking down from the Hall, Elena got a real sense of just how many people were dependent on her husband's leadership, and why he took their safety and well being so seriously.

The morning of the meeting was warm, with cheerful, fluffy clouds in the sky and bright sunshine—not exactly the sort of weather befitting the news Hugh was set to deliver. Because of the massive amount of people, an impromptu meeting site near the Hall was chosen, with the limestone cliffs providing some natural acoustics to carry a speaker's voice out to any listening ears. All told, the final head count was more than twenty score— almost five hundred men, women, all the way down to those who could barely be counted as such. Oswolf was there as a Church witness, and other members of the Hall were also in attendance, Elena, Sybil, Isolda and her husband Gerald, and more. Sybil lingered next to the tall priest, although the two never touched one another directly. John was bound up in a blanket Elena had tied about her waist and shoulder, and she swayed gently with him, soothing him with the rocking motion he liked. He wasn't the only young one there, either—she spotted more than a few mothers carrying children of all ages and sizes.

As ealdorman, Hugh had the right to speak first. Standing tall, dark and imposing, he raised his hands for silence after everyone had gathered together. "Thank you all for coming," he said, as the heavy timbre of his voice carried and the last of the murmuring voices died away. "This Shire Court is now recognized, and my sole purpose of calling you all here is to warn you all, trouble is coming."

Because of the rocks at her back, to Elena, the hum of voices was louder than it would have otherwise been, but Hugh was louder still. "Anyone with working ears has heard the news by now, the Danes, our old enemies, are moving again. A half- dozen cities have already borne the brunt of their attacks, both those near to our shores and others far away. And whether you call Corfe home or not, what happens to it still affects everyone here." Hugh let that hang in the air for a moment, his eyes scanning the crowd, measuring responses, watching faces.

"Well, what do you want us to do about it?" asked one voice.

"I propose we make a defense—here, at Corfe. I know some of you call Swanwich, to the east of us, your home... but I don't believe we can make a stand there." Some of the crowd grumbled and complained loudly at that, but Hugh held up both hands. "Anyone who wishes may bring his family and valuables here to Corfe for safety's sake, and either if—or, more likely, when—the Danes attack and ransack Swanwich, I will do everything in my power to see it repaired and rebuilt, if need be." He let those words sink in, pausing for a moment. "The story goes that, a century ago, over a hundred Danish warships were dashed onto the rocks south of the town. Not a single Dane survived it. If *I* know that story, the Danes will know it as well—perhaps superstition will protect Swanwich better than any force of arms could hope to muster.

"Also, the attacking force may just be few in number, men looking for soft targets, a quick victory, and a rich payday once they escape with any ill-gotten gains they collect." He counted off on his fingers, "Valuables, livestock, women and children for wives, slaves... or worse."

The air was so silent then and it almost felt like a physical weight about Elena's shoulders.

"But that isn't a certain thing—whether the raiders are a scouting party or a mighty host, I propose we must either make a stand here and turn them back... or we must all turn together, and run away."

"Never!" someone said.

"But we aren't soldiers, Milord!" shouted another, a stocky man near the front of the crowd. "I sell milk for a living—livestock I've got, but my cows' got a stronger kick than the likes of me." That earned a few chuckles. "How are men like me supposed to fight soldiers armed to the teeth or better?"

Hugh snapped his fingers, pointing at the milkman. "A fair point... Dodson, wasn't it?"

"Yes, Lord." The man dipped his head respectfully.

"Good, at least I know who I can get my milk from when this is all over," Lord Isarnon said with a little grin. That got a few laughs in response. "Nay, as Friend Dodson says, you aren't soldiers—most of you. Some of us have seen more than our share of battles, but there's no shame in a man knowing his limitations—or woman, for that matter. That's one reason the Court was opened to anyone who cared to attend, women have as much, if not more, to lose in this affair than we men do. It's only right they hear about the risks, and be aware of my proposal in the defense of the town."

Elena saw a few unfriendly faces glaring at Hugh, but none of them spoke up in objection.

"Most of you may know I was on an extended absence earlier this year, one I just recently returned from. Elfhar, Ealdorman of Mercia, requested my presence and I answered him. And I'm sure I don't need to speak here today about just how strong and influential the Prince of Mercia is, do I?"

Another hum, the sound of concurring voices—Elfhar had a reputation far from his own lands.

"Elfhar was the one involved in seeing the body of King Edward moved from Wareham to Shaftesbury Abbey earlier this year, a cause near and dear to his heart. And thus," Hugh continued, "to him, I proposed a trade. In exchange for helping to lay the young King to rest, and assisting him in defending his own lands, he would assist me in defending mine. I've already made preparations for an armed force of Mercian soldiers to arm the fort near Wareham, ready to help us if needed—hundreds of armed, trained soldiers able to come to Corfe's defense at a moment's notice."

Again, Hugh went quiet, letting the force of his words linger, letting his listeners consider that offer. A good many faces that had seemed grim or displeased moments before seemed to brighten, or at least seemed open to a more hopeful outcome. Elena hoped it was a good sign.

"Good people," Hugh said, "as your Lord, this is my proposal: any able-bodied man who wishes it can take up arms as a first line of defense for the town. Elfhar has graciously agreed to provide arms for any man who has need of them. This winter, you will be trained to fight, to march, to defend which is most precious to you: your life, your family's lives, and whatever possessions you hold dearest. When the weather warms again, if the attacking force appears and is few in number, we will drive them back into the sea and make them regret ever coming to our shores." A few men broke out in cheers at that. Hugh waited for the call to die down. "But, whether they are many or few," he continued, "we will make a stand here, and together with Elfhar's superior force, we will make those Danish dogs regret they ever even *thought* about going to sea at all!" There was more cheering, enough that John gave a little start in his mother's arms and started to cry. Elena bent her head and shushed him, soothing his tears away as best she could.

"Are there any objections?" Hugh said. When no one spoke up—either lacking in objections, or in courage—he spoke further, "Anyone who wishes to abstain may speak to me personally on the matter. But, for now, I call an end to this Court. Thank you all for coming. Now, we prepare for battle."

EVERY DAY, Elena looked to the sky in hopes of snow. As each day passed and no snow came, she worried Hugh's prediction might come true—or rather, come too early. The weather was warm and surprisingly pleasant through the rest of October, and even into November and early December until temperatures began to fall and the regular autumn chill set in. Her husband's little army, just over three hundred strong, began to drill and build itself into a proper fighting force, but it was extremely slow going. Hugh kept about a score of armed men in the defense of the Hall, and there were maybe a score more who lived in or around Corfe who'd seen armed combat, so they became officers by sheer necessity. In the way of things, the captains all reported to Oswolf, who then reported to Hugh. Both men weren't above getting their hands dirty and drilling with the men in person, showing them how to march, to hold a spear and shield, how a shield wall was constructed and held in place. It was a marvel to watch them, sometimes, and both men truly seemed to be in their element, as though they'd missed their true calling.

Still, there was no snow, yet no warships were spotted at the coast. On clear days, it was possible to see from Hugh's Hall all the way past Corfe and very nearly to the coastline—rocky cliffs of limestone lined the southern edge of the peninsula, but then stretched out into a rocky beach around the southeastern edge, flattening out even further at the smaller settlement of Swanwich that was due east of Corfe, which meant a great deal of land had to be watched for enemy incursion. The necessities of life required that Elena couldn't simply live on a knife's edge all of the time, always dreading news in anticipation of a report that never came—by the time *Cristes Mæsse* came and went, she was thoroughly exhausted on top of everything else the holiday season required of her.

Snow finally came in early January, and Elena breathed a small sigh of relief when it did. The cold weather felt like a temporary buffer, a shield that covered her home and the entire town—it was a protection of her own imagination, but if Hugh believed that winter would keep the Danes away, she believed him. Even a temporary relief was still a relief. The snow did bring an unexpected arrival, however, and a Danish one at that —Ivan Black-Neck returned, unannounced just like before, seated on his horse with a light dusting of snow on his shoulders. When Hugh went out to meet him, Elena followed behind, wrapped up tight against the chill in the air.

"Iron Hand!" the Dane said with a smile.

"Black-Neck," Hugh answered in a pleasant manner. "You're welcome in my Hall."

"Glad I am to hear it," Ivan said as he dismounted. "It's cold as a seer's black heart out here." The two men clasped forearms in greeting, then Ivan dipped his head to Elena. "Greetings, Lady."

"Ivan, welcome back," she said. "I'll have something warm prepared for you, do come in."

"Thank you." Ivan's horse was taken to the stables, and the three of them went inside. The hearth inside the main room of the Hall was burning bright, with flames dancing higher than she was tall. The two men retreated to Hugh's sitting room while she went to check on her napping boy, and then after removing her shawl and adjusting her skirts to where they were more comfortable and clean of snow, she went to fetch the hot drinks she'd promised.

Ivan was reciting some sort of story or memory of his, laughing uproariously all the while, as Hugh sat to one side with a quiet smile on his face. A hot cup of spiced ale was placed before each of them. "As promised—drink up, please."

"My thanks," Ivan said, taking a deep drink before thinking twice, swallowing quick and taking a deep, cooling inhale. "Odin's beard!" He bent his back with a sharp coughing fit, slapping his chest until the fit passed. "I suppose... I deserved that."

"Mm." Hugh smirked and took a much smaller, lighter sip of the hot beverage. "Elena, sit. I think you might want to hear what our friend here has to share."

Elena looked surprised, but she took a seat next to Hugh as instructed, settling her skirts into place, taking one of his hands in hers.

The Dane had recovered by that time, and he, too, took a

much smaller sip. "You're a strange man, Hugh, I'll grant you that much. I've known a jarl or two in my time who'd sooner cut their own throats than talk politics with women about. They say it's bad luck."

"Then it's a good thing I'm not a jarl, I suppose," Hugh said, waving a hand. "I told you all about how Elena was involved when I had to choose who my vote would be for the next king—whether by happenstance or Providence, she's intimately aware of the events surrounding Æthelred's rise to the throne, and of his mother's involvement in getting him there. And, I daresay, my wife's proven herself to be more than smart and capable enough to handle herself, when necessary. You can speak freely on these matters."

Elena did feel a little surge of pride at her husband's words, but she tried not to let it show on her face. She did give his hand a squeeze in thanks, however.

Ivan raised his cup in a salute, took a sip, and leaned back. "From what I'm told, Winchester—which is, to say, the King and his doting mother—are quite unhappy with you throwing your lot in with Elfhar and joining me in our little excursion into the Welsh countryside last year."

Hugh nodded. "I expected as much. I also haven't been called to serve by the King since he took the throne more than three years ago, so I'm well aware of his opinion of me right now." He took a sip of his drink and offered Elena the cup, she shook her head.

"Just so." Ivan nodded, taking another drink. "But Elfhar's been told, for the sake of appearances, the boy-king won't move against you out in the open—there's too many of the noble types who know and respect the name and word of Hugh the Iron Hand. You being so close to the boy's father is likely the explanation for that."

Again, Hugh nodded. This time, he didn't answer—King Edgar's death was still a tender subject for him, years later.

"It sounds like they'll leave you to sweat with the wolves creeping at your door, assuming my brethren do show up to pay your people a visit. Once that's over, Æthelred hasn't lost a single man or shilling to his name, and Elfrida gets the satisfaction of watching Lord Isarnon grovel and beg for assistance." Black-Neck shrugged, spreading his hands. "No offense intended, Lord, but you can hardly fault them, either you dance on their strings, or they don't have to lift a finger to defend a noble they can't keep under their thumb. Either way, it's a victory."

"Mm." Hugh's grunt was less amused that time. "Æthelred's not an enemy I wanted to make... but I'm unsure how to handle him any other way."

"My people are known to say it's better to die with honor than live with shame, friend Hugh." Ivan took his cup and drank it down, chugging the warm liquor with greedy gulps, then wiping his blond mustache clean.

"Not the most... comforting of sayings," Elena noted, scrunching up her nose.

The Dane grinned. "Granted, Lady. But one to live by, all the same."

"Be that as it may," Hugh said, "I don't intend to die yet. I intend to make a stand here, and with your and Elfhar's help, I think we have a good chance at success."

"Well said!" Ivan clapped the table, a grin on his face. "I look forward to seeing your regulars in action." Given the eager shine in his eyes, Elena wondered just what the immediate future held for Corfe's little ragtag army, but she hoped it was a promising sign of things to come.

A PROMISE OF BATTLE

*T*he winter season was short-lived. By early March, the last snow was gone and the winter chill wasn't far behind. It was an inevitable fact spring would have to come, but Elena witnessed its arrival with dread all the same.

Corfe's little battalion had not wasted those cold months idling about—what started as an inept, ragtag group of conscripts had shaped itself into a proper, albeit small, army of sorts. Hugh, Oswolf and the rest of the officers spent the weeks planning and preparing for most contingencies they could think up. Since an attack was likely to come from either the south or the east and the available number of horses was small in number, the defenders divided their number in two, each of them practicing moving as a single unit across the terrain—marching, running, carrying round, wooden shields almost half as long as some of the men were tall. They learned the art of the shield wall, erecting a barrier of wood and bristling steel that would block enemy arrows, or even the charge of soldiers and riders. The men would wrap their spears in thick leather to dull the blows and practice hurling themselves at one another, building strength and discipline for what everyone assumed would be the battle to come.

A network of guard posts and messengers was set up along the coast every half-mile, from the southernmost tip of the peninsula all the way to Swanwich Bay. Two men with horses would watch the waters and prepare to quit their post if they spotted a large number of ships approaching the coast. Once the scouts arrived, a pair of messengers would be sent to Wareham to raise the alarm with Ivan Black-Neck and his men, urging them to return to Corfe as soon as possible. Black-Neck had two whole battalions of mounted soldiers at his beck and call, which was sure to turn the tide in their favor.

Since the town lacked the resources to man a standing army, the threat of Danish raiding parties was as much of a blessing as it was a curse—those townsmen who were willing to fight and defend their homes gained an invaluable lesson in warfare, and a chance to learn how to defend themselves. But the unspoken promise of those raiders appearing was always on a man's mind, though perhaps not always spoken of aloud, as though just mentioning them might summon a fleet of ships into existence.

When Ivan visited Corfe over the winter months, he watched the preparations with an interested eye and a professional soldier's curiosity, but he was often away—either managing his men at the fort at Wareham, several miles to the north, or otherwise occupied with the business of his lord. Elena understood that other matters sometimes took precedence over her little corner of the world, but it was difficult to bite her tongue—war was a man's job, and she simply had to grit her teeth and wait, every single day, wondering if the lingering sensation of doom hanging over her head would ever drop.

On the 24th of March, a day before her son's first birthday, it did.

The morning was unnaturally cool just before dawn, but the

sun was hidden that morning as a thick fog bank swept over the region, so thick in places it seemed more like smoke. The air grew brighter, but there was no sun, nothing beyond a gradual transition of grey shades in the air around Hugh's Hall and the town in the distance. Elena slept fitfully the night prior, on account of how little John seemed not to want to sleep at all. By the time the fog was bright enough to consider it morning, Elena was catching another catnap when there was a loud banging on her bedroom door.

Sybil was waiting for her, with the little boy tucked tight against her hip. "There's been word, Milady."

Elena rubbed her eyes. "Word? What word?"

The maidservant licked her lips. "They're here, Milady, your husband was right. The Danes have finally come."

THE LADY of Corfe had little role to play in the battle herself. The waiting was the worst part, but Elena supposed, given how much of that she'd been subjected to over the last few months, she could withstand a little more. The women and children who could, had taken shelter inside the Hall's protective walls, but since every sword- and spear-arm available was needed, the Hall was left almost completely unguarded—only the men who couldn't join the fight below remained behind, a skeleton force at best.

In truth, the Hall offered the best view of the battlefield one could get, and over the top of the barricaded southern gates, Elena could look down the slope of the hill to the town and the field beyond it, as the fog seemed to have cleared just enough so she could see the men gathering beyond the last cluster of huts at Corfe's periphery, both to the east and the south. The two groups of armed defenders stood like hulking, spined tortoises, waiting, peering through the gloom to see where their attackers might come from.

For an hour or longer, they waited—everyone, from the host gathered atop the hill, to the men at the base of it. No fires or torches were lit to better keep their numbers concealed, but it was likely the enemy was doing the same thing. All the while, Elena kept her eyes focused southward. She couldn't spot which of the figures mounted on horseback was her husband, but Elena hardly dared to blink or take a breath as she, and the whole world around her, waited.

The shape of the invaders emerged out of the mist like a laborious beast, rolling with long arms out of the murk. The Danes came with a great, wordless roar of marching men, beating their weapons against their round shields. At the sight of them, a horn began to blow from the southern force, and Elena heard the solitary sound of a child's mournful wailing in reply. The southern force built up their wall in a long row, single-file, spears turned outward, waiting for the Danes to reach their line. From a distance, she watched the eastern defenders pick up and march together, double-time, hurrying to reach their brethren before the raiders did. The men seemed to move in slow motion to Elena's rapt eyes. All the while, the raiding force grew in size and numbers, as more and more men rose out of the mist and ran forward to the attack.

"Too slow," she said, under her breath. Her heart was pounding, burning, but she knew it was still true—the eastern defenders wouldn't reach the southern line in time.

The crash of men against men was so loud that everyone atop the hill heard the sound of it. The line of shields seemed to shudder, and it nearly broke in two or three places at once; as some men fell, others closed in around them, keeping their defense up. The mounted men rode up and down the line, shouting, calling, at times jumping from the saddle to plug a hole in the line before it could break. Still more of the raiders came— hundreds more. Hugh had been wrong about the small size of the attacking force, very wrong indeed. Elena's throat was parched, dry as a fistful of hot ash, but she couldn't turn away. Nobody in the yard could.

There was a feeble attempt at a few cheers when the eastern force reached the southern line, still running. Some shored up the nearest flank, while more ran in single-file behind the southern line. Then they pushed forward, adding their shields to the others, relieving some who were wounded or too tired to keep up the fighting. Now reinforced, the single line held and seemed stronger for the moment, but by that time it was obvious the Danes outnumbered the English by better than two or even three to one.

After several more minutes, a momentary lull came over the battlefield. Although the shield wall remained, the Danes broke off the attack for a moment, dragging the bodies of their dead and wounded away. The shield wall parted in places for the defenders to do the same. Elena could hear women weeping, and little wonder. It was too far away to see the faces of the fallen, but for some gathered on the hill, they would never speak to the men they loved, the fathers they depended on, ever again. Elena dared to close her eyes for the briefest of moments, whisper a prayer that, somehow, more of their number would be wounded rather than dead.

John squirmed in her arms, and Elena started. She had to ease her grip on him before the tension in her very bones caused her to hurt him, but she didn't dare let him go. Where were Ivan Black-Neck and his men? Surely the Danes would overwhelm the English when they charged again.

There was some shouting, some words being exchanged at the bottom of the hill, but she couldn't make them out. It was the way of men to be braggadocious. She could imagine the raiders taunting the pitiful defending force, shouting about what those men intended to do to the women and children they found, once the men of Corfe were dead or scattered on the field. A raucous guffaw filled the air above the enemy horde. Elena could see crows gathering, their black wings fluttering above the heads of the two armies. When they had their chances, the carrion birds would land and feast on whatever they could find, an image that made Elena want to close her eyes.

But she couldn't. Her husband was down there—with God's grace, he might even be alive.

Whatever the outcome, she could not turn away.

The Danes pushed forward to finish off the defenders. Given the size of their host, they pushed out in a crescent formation, intent on swallowing up the single line of soldiers and chew them to pieces. Elena's heart froze in her chest as she stood silent, waiting for the end.

And then, a miraculous thing happened. Another horn began to blow.

Then two horns. Then three.

"Look!" someone shouted.

Men on horseback appeared at the top of the cliffs on either side of Hugh's Hall, carrying torches that burned away the clinging fog. Still more riders appeared from out of the west, a force dozens, even hundreds strong—their swords were up and in their hands, and more horns blew a blast as they rode down upon the Danish horde. The attackers, who'd pushed forward so steadily just moments earlier, wavered and began to break in seconds as the riders smashed through the sides of their line and went straight through, out the other side, leaving mangled and shattered men behind.

The Danes turned and fled. As a crazed monster they'd appeared, but now they scattered and melted away like rats before a storm.

The sound of everyone in the yard gave such a cry that it made Elena's ears ring from the force of it, and her shout was as loud as any of them. John clapped both of his hands over his ears.

A group of horsemen were riding near the base of the cliffs, heading for the stake wall surrounding the yard. It was possible to spot the top of Ivan Black-Neck's yellow head, to see he was riding towards the Hall to come with what she hoped was good news.

"Open the gate!" Elena ordered.

Several moments later, Ivan rode in with several of his men—the Dane was head and shoulders taller than any of them, and their drab English garb and uniforms clashed with his long beard and its rattling decor.

"Lady Elena," he said, bowing from the waist.

"Aside from my husband, you're the best sight I've seen all day," she answered, hearing a few laughs from the crowd.

"As a conciliatory prize, I'll accept that." Ivan grinned. "Apologies for our delay in getting here, Milady. It's easy to get turned around and around in weather like this." He cast an eye skyward, spitting into the dirt in disgust.

"So..." Elena licked her lips. "What you're saying is you got lost on the way here."

"Indeed so."

"Did it not occur to you, good sir, to perhaps stop and ask for directions?"

Ivan seemed to consider that. "Well... we did find our way here eventually, Milady."

IN ALL, nearly a thousand of the enemy had taken the field—of that number, nearly a quarter were dead upon it. Their bodies were piled up, far away from the city, put to the torch and left to burn. Corfe's forces, being smaller, had also lost a smaller number, but in all more than a score were dead, and twice that many were wounded. It was a sad thing, knowing so many families had lost someone dear to them.

Hugh and Oswolf, by some miracle, were unscathed, save for

a sizable knot on the side of the Scot's enormous head where he'd caught the blunt end of an English spear by accident. Elena was overjoyed when her Lord appeared on the hill with his friend, coming back to the Hall at last. She heard Sybil weeping with happiness when the oversized priest embraced her, and Elena had to admit she shed a few tears herself when Hugh took her in his arms.

The next few days were tense ones, even with the knowledge that Ivan's soldiers had harried the Danes all the way back to their ships, jeering and shouting at the raiders as those who'd escaped to their ships took to sea and sailed away for faraway shores—or so Elena hoped, anyway. Although more scouts were posted and watched the horizon of the southern seas with anticipation in the days following the attack, the Danes did not return. Swanwich was spared, thankfully, since the Danes had landed on the southern beaches; perhaps Hugh's suspicions hadn't all been wrong, after all.

The fallen were gathered and buried in the cemetery of the parish church. Oswolf oversaw every single one of the burials, tirelessly ushering their souls off to the Hereafter without complaint, and shared tales of the men's bravery, even in the face of what might have seemed as certain defeat. Hugh offered a small stipend to each family of the dead men, and as much support as could be spared for the rest of the survivors. It was planting season, and now that the battle was over, those still remaining would have to work even harder to pick up the slack of those who'd paid the ultimate price to defend their home.

SLOWLY, life began to return to normal. Then, in the second week of April, a messenger appeared at the northern gate. He was on a horse and alone, but said he bore a message for the Lord Isarnon and refused to speak on the matter further. Hugh went out to meet the man, heard the message, then bid the rider good day and sent him on his way. Watching from the Hall, Elena could see a look on her husband's face that she recognized all too well. Trouble.

"Hugh, what is it?"

He pressed his lips to a thin line and rubbed one bearded cheek. "You're not going to like it," he said.

"With a warning like that, I scarcely doubt it. What is it?"

"That was a messenger," he said, nodding his head in the direction of the northern gate.

"Yes, so I gathered."

"From the King."

She blinked.

"Æthelred is paying us a visit in two days' time." He blew out a low, soft breath. "And Elfrida is coming with him."

AN ENDING AND A NEW BEGINNING

The day of the King's arrival was spoken of by the townsfolk for many a year afterward, given the fanfare and excitement once the word got out. Most still remembered when Elfrida visited Hugh's Hall some years prior, back before becoming the Queen Regent; some might have even known that Æthelred was with her as well, bound to his mother's side as surely as if he'd worn a chain around his neck. Very few knew the real intent behind their visit, or how King Edward had made a surprise visit before he was assassinated by Elfrida's coterie—the maneuver had put political pressure on Hugh for not supporting Æthelred's claim to the throne from the outset, pressure that hadn't let up even years later.

Elena still harbored a deep resentment for Elfrida after all that time, and she was in no mood to prepare her house for any such guests, but she did so anyway without complaint, telling herself it was for Hugh's benefit, not to satisfy either the Queen or the young King dancing at the end of her leash. The whole town was in an uproar, but for her part, she made sure Hugh's Hall was tastefully decorated. Even though the food stores were low, she, along with Isolda and the remaining kitchen staff's help, managed to put together a menu fit for any Winchester banquet hall. It was a relief the visit came in springtime, which meant there would be time to restock those stores before the next winter.

The royal procession came to Corfe by way of Wareham, circling around to enter the town by the eastern road. It might have been the first time for some to ever see the King, and might be the last time in their lives to ever see him. Æthelred was a young man by that time, rather than the doe-eyed boy he'd been during his last visit, with longer hair and a face dotted with acne. Elfrida was the same, cold-eyed beauty Elena remembered—her blonde hair was bound up in braids atop her head, but her dress likely cost more than the whole town through which she was riding. Both of the monarchs wore their crowns openly, waving politely for the crowd who came out to wave and cheer for them. It was an ostentatious sort of display, one that Elena was sure satisfied the Queen Regent immensely.

The retinue riding with the royal mother and son was even larger in number than the last time they'd visited the Hall, and finding a spot for everyone proved to be a challenge. Æthelred had the seat of honor, while Elfrida sat next to the King with Hugh, Elena, and John, while the remaining diners gathered around the rest of the tables; the group had been riding steadily all morning, and most of them were famished. A number of townsfolk were invited as well, some notable figures who'd made a name for themselves during what was being colloquially called "The Battle at Kingston Hill", named after the wide field south of the town. Oswolf was there, seated next to Ivan Black-Neck, and the two were chatting about the subject of religion in fervent, passionate tones—the priest appeared to be working hard to save the Dane's soul by any means necessary, which appeared to amuse Black-Neck to no end. Elena wore her best dress, and the silver brooch Hugh had specially made for her as a gift which bore the black enamel starling in honor of the sobriquet Hugh had given her so long ago, and a pair of figures carved into the silver face, holding a pale blue gem. Still, she did feel a touch overdressed, given that she was doing her best to coax her toddler to eat some mashed apples with limited success.

"Oh, he is precious," she heard a familiar voice say. Looking over her shoulder, she saw the Queen eyeing her with a small uptick of a smile at the corner of her mouth; Elena might have called it *patronizing* if she wasn't carefully, carefully guarding her emotions where it came to Elfrida. The Queen Regent had a beauty as cold as a deep winter's morning—she was pleasant to look at, with wide cheekbones, a sharp chin and eyes that could pin someone to the floor with a hard glare. Elena remembered feeling very inadequate, even ugly, the first time she'd properly met Elfrida after her husband died. Now, she felt no such humility or genuflection. She'd seen the depths of cruelty Elfrida could stoop to and Elena refused to shrink before the woman ever again.

Yet, she could still be polite. For Hugh's sake, anyway. "Thank you, Majesty," Elena said.

"How old is he?"

"He turned a year several weeks ago."

"Really!" Elfrida leaned over towards John, who stared back with his wide eyes, mouth slightly agape, still stained with food. "We congratulate you, little one," she said.

John, appearing to think very little of the Queen's tidings, gave a wet-sounding burp.

Elfrida sat back with a little laugh. "And spirited, too. I shall see to it that he's sent a gift worthy of an ealdorman's son."

"Thank you," Elena said again. She wanted to say more, to ask all of the questions that had burned themselves into her heart since that day, years ago—why Elfrida conspired to kill her stepson, whether she thought King Edgar would have approved, if the throne was really worth the price of Æthelred watching his brother being murdered before his eyes—but Elena said nothing. What could she say, really? Elfrida appeared to be quite satisfied with her current lot in life, and nothing Elena could have done or said would change that.

As though fated, Elfrida sat back and looked thoughtful for a moment. She took a sip of her drink and smiled again at Elena. "We heard the news of your pregnancy and your son's birth with great interest, given how long you waited to bear children at all. You, too, are to be congratulated, my dear. Isn't it amazing, what a woman will go through for the benefit of her child?" The Queen Regent raised her glass to Elena in salute. It was such a small, innocent-looking gesture, but the gleam in the woman's eye made Elena's blood run cold.

Elena was quite certain Elfrida hadn't lost a wink of sleep over her stepson's fate.

"Yes, of course. And thank you, Your Majesty." Elena coughed, clearing her throat as she went back to feeding John. "Will you and the King be staying with us long?"

"I shouldn't think so," Elfrida answered, setting her cup aside. "In fact, I'm quite certain we'll be moving on after my son has eaten his fill."

"Truly?" Elena nearly dropped the wooden spoon in surprise. John shook his arms, chasing after it as he babbled something.

"Quite so," the Queen answered. Her smile was gone, and she looked contemplative, thoughtful again. "His Majesty's destination is the larger towns of Cornwall and Exanceaster, my childhood home, in the hopes of seeing for himself just how much damage the Danish invaders managed to cause." There was a subtext to that statement, something in-between the lines of what was said, but Elena would've staked her claim on the fact Elfrida seemed almost displeased that Corfe had managed to evade the same fate that had befallen other larger, even better-defended towns.

Elena kept her voice as pleasantly neutral as possible. "Then, pray, I hope you'll bid my hopes of a pleasant and safe journey to His Majesty?" she said with a contented smile.

Elfrida's eyes widened just so as she smiled, the barest hint of anything at all, but it was enough. "Of course, my dear."

The feast wound down after that, and after thanking Lord Isarnon for his hospitality and that of his Hall, King Æthelred announced his company was departing. Hugh, in turn, thanked the King for visiting and wished him, the Queen Regent, and their assembly good health and—as Elena had—a safe journey. Elena was never so relieved as when the last of them mounted their horses and left by way of the northern gate to find the road that would lead them west.

With any luck, it would be the last that any of them ever saw of Æthelred or Elfrida. Elena prayed it would be so.

Ivan Black-Neck remained, looking quite pleased with the goings-on. He and Oswolf took offered seats at the Lord's table, while Hugh and Elena lingered. Most of the guests were still eating their fill, enjoying the bounty that Hugh offered—free food was free food, after all.

"Whatever *did* you say to the Queen, Milady?" Ivan asked.

"Mm?" Elena had given up trying to feed her son anything else, and let him play on the floor, gnawing on a carved wooden teething toy. John wasn't up to walking yet, but he continuously crawled everywhere, and she had to fetch him if he strayed too far. "In regard to what?"

The Dane lowered his voice in a conspiratorial tone. "I haven't seen her look that unhappy since Æthelred turned fourteen—it's already being whispered that she's trying to keep a tight hold on his reins, even while he's tiring of her interference and looking to put her out to pasture for good."

Elena sniffed. "I simply made it known I wished her and the King a pleasant journey, that's all."

Oswolf snorted. "I s'pose 'tis a more prettier speech than jus' sayin' 'Get'cha gone'."

"It will be my *immense* pleasure if the Queen Regent and her son never darken our doorstep again," Elena said.

"Peace, Wife," Hugh said softly, but he didn't disagree, either.

Elena harrumphed and stayed quiet.

"I would say you're to be congratulated, Lord," Ivan said, dipping his head respectfully. "You managed to evade the Queen's pitfalls quite expertly, but after today's meeting, nobody will ever believe it."

"No?" Hugh sounded resigned, but curious all the same.

"Nay, Lord." Ivan shook his head. "It's victors that write the histories, I'm told, and for now Elfrida still has a firm grip on those reins I mentioned. By the time Æthelred shakes her loose, Corfe and Kingston Hill will be a distant memory. I'm not sure if anyone will ever remember what you and your people accomplished here."

"Let them remember, or let them forget," Hugh said with a shrug. "I care little for either. I did what I had to for my people, my wife, and my son—that will have to be enough."

"Hear, hear," Oswolf said, raising his cup in a toast.

Ivan did the same in silent affirmation. Elena, on a whim, followed suit. John babbled, adding his vote as well.

Hugh drained his cup, then drummed the tabletop with both hands. "Well Os, are you ready?"

"Ready f'what, Milord?" Oswolf said, taking a fresh drink from his glass.

The Lord Isarnon nodded to the door behind the priest. "For that."

Oswolf turned around to where Sybil was standing in the doorway. She wore a white-and-cream colored dress Elena had happily provided for the occasion, hemmed and mended for the taller, bustier woman. A garland of anemone flowers was in her hair, bound in a black braid, with the rest falling in a loose drape down her back. She was holding a small bouquet of white and yellow hyacinths, and looking right at Oswolf. "Finally caught you," she said with a smirk.

In response, Oswolf promptly choked on his drink.

Elena, who'd planned the reveal right down to the detail and the time of day, with the afternoon sunlight flowing into the Hall, was satisfactorily smug at Oswolf's reaction.

SO FATHER OSWOLF, parish priest of Corfe, was married to Sybil, head servant of the Isarnon household. Married clergymen weren't unheard of in those days, after all, and even though the Scot looked a little wild-eyed at having been so unexpectedly cornered into his nuptials, he did seem quite happy with the outcome. Sybil, for her part, cried like a little girl all through the ceremony, which Hugh officiated since there wasn't another priest to be found for miles, and the Lord had determined his old friend had avoided the subject of marriage for quite long enough.

The end result seemed satisfactory to everyone, and the feast once intended for the King's visit now served double-duty as a reception feast for the happy couple. Elena was sure it couldn't have ended on a better note than that one.

Except there was just one thing left for her to do.

A GOOD LIFE

*N*ight came, as it always did. John was, thankfully, asleep in his bed, quite exhausted from the events of that day, even snoring a little.

Elena, on the other hand, sat in hers, quite awake and almost preternaturally alert. "Hugh?"

"Mm?" Hugh was sitting on a bench next to the bed, taking his time getting undressed. He seemed tired again, after the momentous events of the day, but he'd seemed tired ever since the day of the battle. It was another reminder that the grey in his hair wasn't just for the sake of appearances. That made her a little sad to see it.

Sitting in bed, already undressed, she hugged her knees to her chest and stared at him for a moment, watching him move, observing him. They'd come through a great deal together, years of heartache and happiness, the multiple succession of kings, the ambition of ruthless queens, and even bloodshed and war, and survived all of it. It was a poignant moment, one she intended to remember for a long time to come.

"I love you, you know," she said, feeling very small.

Hugh looked up and smiled. "I do know it, starling. I love you too. Do *you* know that?"

Elena nodded, struck to uncomfortable silence for the moment.

When he finished undressing and got up, Hugh took a seat on her side of the bed and opened his arms—he didn't say anything; he never had to. Elena scrambled into the safety of his arms, pressing her face to his shoulder, the warm curve of his neck. She felt safe. She could close her eyes, sigh, savor the feel of his flesh and the heat of his heart as it covered her completely.

"I need that," she said, whispering. "I need you. If something had happened to you that day—"

"But *nothing* did," he said, cutting her off with a gentle finality, like a silk-wrapped blade. "A few scratches, here and there, but nothing worse." His kiss was tender, loving, so very good.

It ended, and she looked up at him, not knowing how to say what she had to say. So, she just said it, "I'm pregnant again."

He scratched his chin, squinted down at her and nodded. "Yes."

Elena blinked. "What? That's all you have to say?"

Hugh had a smug looking smirk on his face. "What would you have me say, Elena? Or should I be surprised, simply for your benefit?"

The response was so beyond what she'd expected that Elena almost went slack-jawed. "You mean you already *knew*?"

He gave her a long, deadpan look. "My Lady, I'm *sure* we had a conversation on this topic not too long ago. Something about 'seeing every inch of your person in a state of undress', I believe."

The gleam in Hugh's eye and wicked smirk on his face was enough to make Elena go red, all over. "T-that may be, but—"

"So." He stopped her, leaning towards the pillows, and Elena was forced to go with him until she was on her back, and he was leering down at her. "Since we're in agreement that I know my wife's body as well as anyone..." He leaned in closer, began kissing across the width of her collarbone; his beard scratched ever so delicately at her tender flesh, while one hand cupped her breast, swirling the nipple with his forefinger. "Then what sort of husband would I be..." That accursed forefinger did just enough to light the spark in her chest, and it followed the trail of his fingers as they slid down her ribs and belly—a belly that was just now beginning to show again. "If I didn't pay attention to those sorts of changes?" He laid his hand flat on her stomach and raised his head, showing that dark, gentle smile she knew so well. "I know you've been wearing your mended dresses again, the ones you wore when you were pregnant with John. I know the signs, the different look you have. You shine, did you know that?"

Elena did know that.

"And didn't I tell you once I was willing to wait for you and more children, if it ever came to that?"

"I do remember," Elena said with a loving smile and a hand on his cheek. "It was the night of *Cristes Mæsse*, before John was born." Then she broke the spell for a moment, flailing both arms. "B-but I didn't think it would *actually* happen!"

Hugh bent his head, and it took her a moment to realize he was laughing, trying to smother the sound of it before it woke the little boy sleeping on the other side of the room. When he raised his head, his eyes were crinkled from the force of his smile. "My dear, dear Elena. Such a woman you've become. And one I'm so, so thankful to call mine."

Elena felt the sting of gleeful tears in her eyes. Reaching up, wrapping her fingers in his hair, she pulled her husband down close, kissing him again as if all the joy, happiness and exuberance in her had to be released before she burst into a thousand pieces.

He gave a contented hum against her mouth, swirling his tongue around with hers, before it turned into a growl of hunger, of desire. He pushed her wrists up above her head and pressed them down into the bed. It made her gasp against his lips, but the spark which had started to lull itself back to sleep, after having nothing but loving kisses and words, woke again with renewed ardor.

"Do you want me?" she asked, her own voice turned darker, hungrier.

"God, yes," he answered, already climbing onto the bed after her.

She opened her legs for him, the soft cleft of flesh he lusted for—the thing she knew he wanted most and she gave it to him without resisting, gladly. Curling her fingers over the hands pinning them down, she dug in with her nails, but not enough to sting him. She sucked her lower lip between her teeth as she watched him lower his hips, saw his swollen prick hanging lower and lower, felt the hot tip of him sear her swollen lower lips like the sweetest firebrand. Elena wanted him to impale her, to drive his flesh into her and fill her up in one hard, wonderful thrust, but he didn't do that. His eyes moved back up to her face, and he showed off that evil, incorrigible smirk of his as he—with slow, deliberate, agonizing slowness—penetrated her. A little at a time, he gave her more of himself. Shallow thrusts became deeper, little by little. At the first touch, Elena squirmed; after the first inch, she whimpered; halfway there and she rolled her head back, daring to moan aloud. "More," she begged. "Please more." She curled her ankles around his muscled legs, trying to pull him closer to her, to fill her up even more, but he was as unshakable as a stone pillar. The man was going to take her in his own way, and she was helpless, just the loving tool he used for his own pleasure.

Hugh gave a wicked little chuckle and never said a word. God, he could be such a bastard at times... but then, he knew just how to handle her, and sometimes waiting was the sweetest torment, and the greatest reward.

That teasing continued, shallow caresses inside of her that

only made her ache and want more, and it seemed like more was the one thing he didn't want to give her. Elena felt a cold shiver of sweat breaking out all over her body, which suddenly went white-out when he, as if sensing her weakest moment, pushed forward with all of his weight. Going from sweet, miserable emptiness to absolute fullness made her open her eyes wide and shriek as if she'd been shot, and the only thing that saved them was Hugh clapping a hand over her mouth to muffle her outcry. Their eyes met for a long, panicked moment, then they both looked over his shoulder, into the shadows at the far end of the room.

All was silent. Nothing stirred.

The Iron Hand turned back, giving her a look between bewildered amusement and disbelief. "You scared me for a second there," he whispered.

"It would've served you right if he woke up, too!" she hissed, but the look on his face was too much. Elena let her head fall back again as she started laughing, shaking all over from the force of it. Hugh didn't resist when she coiled her limbs around him, drawing him back down closer to her, pressing gentle kisses all over his face. The feel of his cock inside of her, so heavy and hard, made for a wonderful contrast to her whispering kisses.

"Perhaps you *might* consider being a touch quieter, starling?" Her husband sounded amused when he suggested it.

"Mmm," she said, sliding one bare leg along the back of his thigh and over the curve of his bottom. "Perhaps the boy needs his *own* room to sleep in. There'll be a second Isarnon newborn coming soon, after all." Elena looked up at his face, love and residual lust shining in her eyes. "And *you* have a job to finish, my Lord."

Hugh chuckled again and didn't need to be told twice. His hands seemed especially greedy that night, roaming over her body, from her breasts to the soft halves of her ass which often bore far too many of his affectionate bruises. He didn't tease her again, but gave in to his hunger, the desire she knew he always carried for her. It was a blessing their bed didn't creak, given how well and thoroughly he pounded into her, how willing she was to take him, how they moved and slid together in a harmony rarely found between two lovers. He was the perfect match for her, a fact she only realized after far too many years, but now she was almost gleeful every time he made love to her— it was love, the truest, purest sort that a man could give to a woman.

Elena held him tight, or as tight as she could, and the familiar sense of his release—the way his breath caught for a moment, the tightness of his body, the look of perfect pain on his face, the feeling of him spilling over inside of her—seemed all so perfect, somehow. She shivered with a pleasure all too similar to an orgasm, but somehow felt even stronger, unlike anything else she could put a name to. The mixture of emotions and feelings swirling in her, from pleasure, to passion, to relief, happiness, joyful sorrow, satisfaction, they all congealed and made her want to burst into song, or weep with happiness. Instead, she stroked her cheek against his when his head fell to her shoulder, and began repeating the words, "I love you, I love you, I love you" over and over again.

Listening to him breathing, feeling his comforting weight atop her body, she went silent for a few moments. All was quiet, all was still.

Perfection.

But it couldn't last forever. "Hugh?" she said, softly.

"Mm?" Hugh sounded sleepy, drugged after their passionate embrace.

"Do you remember asking me once, if I was happy?"

There was a moment of silence. He kissed up her neck, her cheek, to the smooth pass of her brow. "Yes, love. I've asked you that several times, if memory serves."

"Yes. Thank you for caring about that. I'm glad my being happy mattered to you."

"My dearest, starling." He looked down at her, hand against her cheek. "It *always* mattered to me."

"I know that now." Sniffing, feeling new tears and not caring if they fell, Elena smiled and nuzzled his palm. "Thank you, Hugh. For everything."

"Of course, Elena." Hugh Isarnon kissed her again, then slid off of her, gathering the blankets up to cover them both. "Now, let's get some sleep while we can. Tomorrow's bound to be another busy day."

She didn't disagree, her life with the Iron Hand was most definitely busy. With one child now and another on the way, she was sure her life would never *not* be busy ever again.

It was a good life. Elena was thankful for it. Together with her husband—with her family—she resolved to enjoy it to its fullest.

The End

NOTE FROM THE AUTHOR

Almost ten years ago, a writer friend of mine talked about a story she was working on, about a domineering man and the woman caught in his clutches. If Elena Isarnon had a birthday, it was that date, for it spawned a story seed of my own, only in reverse: *she* was the strong-willed, stubborn one, and her husband Hugh was the quiet man in love with her.

All these years later, I feel like I can safely say that Elena and Hugh's story is fully and completely told—I'll never say never, but I hope I've given my little English family the Happily Ever After that they richly deserve. I've grown to love these characters, more than I originally ever expected to, and I'm honored by every single person who took the time to buy these books, read these stories, and to share their opinion when they reviewed them. Thank you to every single person who became a part of my story for just a little while.

Also, I'd like to give thanks to Martyn Whittock for writing *A Brief History of Life in the Middle Ages* (Robinson Publishing, 2009), which I found very useful as reference material, and to Maria Mendes for the absolutely critical and expert childbirth advice. I'm eternally in her debt, and so very thankful for her guidance.

AYCEE MASTERSON

I've been writing for more than two decades, and professionally published for a number of years. I also previously contributed to the writing troupe Blushing Mischief. You can find my Blushing page at https://www.blushingbooks.com/brand/aycee-masterson/

I live in the Southern US, have far too many children running around to find time to do much of anything, yet I keep dreaming about characters and their stories, and keep doing my best to share those stories as much as I can. I hope you find something you like in what I write, and that you'll find a way to share it with me.

I can be found on Twitter at @ayceemasterson. Happy reading!

You can find a splash page with all of my books at the following link: https://ayceemastersonbooks.wordpress.com/books/

My Blushing author page can be found at https://www.blushingbooks.com/brand/aycee-masterson/

I can be found on Twitter at @ayceemasterson. Happy reading!

Don't miss these exciting titles by Aycee Masterson and Blushing Books:

Iron Hand's Bride series
The Iron Hand's Bride (books 1 and 2)
The Lady and the Iron Hand (book 3)

Single titles
Dreams in the Dust
The Gold and the Gunner

Anthologies
The 12 Naughty Days of Christmas 2020

BLUSHING BOOKS

Blushing Books is the oldest eBook publisher on the web. We've been running websites that publish steamy romance and erotica since 1999, and we have been selling eBooks since 2003. We have free and promotional offerings that change weekly, so please do visit us at http://www.blushingbooks.com/free.

BLUSHING BOOKS NEWSLETTER

Please join the Blushing Books newsletter
to receive updates & special promotional offers.
You can also join by using your mobile phone:
Just text BLUSHING to 22828.

Every month, one new sign up via text messaging will receive a
$25.00 Amazon gift card, so sign up today!